VIRGINIA CREEPER
THE MYSTERY HOUSE SERIES, BOOK TEN

Eva Pohler

Copyright © 2023 by Eva Pohler.

All rights reserved. No part of this publication may be reproduced, distributed or transmitted in any form or by any means, including photocopying, recording, or other electronic or mechanical methods, without the prior written permission of the publisher, except in the case of brief quotations embodied in critical reviews and certain other noncommercial uses permitted by copyright law. For permission requests, write to the publisher, addressed "Attention: Permissions Coordinator," at the address below.

Eva Pohler Books
20011 Park Ranch
San Antonio, Texas 78259
www.evapohler.com

Publisher's Note: This is a work of fiction. Names, characters, places, and incidents are a product of the author's imagination. Locales and public names are sometimes used for atmospheric purposes. Any resemblance to actual people, living or dead, or to businesses, companies, events, institutions, or locales is completely coincidental.

Copy Editor: Alexis Rigoni

Book Cover Design by B Rose DesignZ

VIRGINIA CREEPER/ Eva Pohler. -- 1st ed.

Paperback ISBN: 9798370584947

Contents

The House on Kestrel Court 3
A Paranormal Investigation 13
The Second Night 24
The Shed 34
A Secret Crypt 43
Return to Williamsburg 52
The Ghost Tour and the Creeper 61
The Ghosts of Peyton   Randolph House 71
Hamilton 81
Eve 95
Crossings 103
Sam Dickenson 120
The Busch Gardens Incident 129
The Monster 137
Mr. Murphy's Wine Cellar 148
Jacinda Bloom 155
Jolly Pond 161
The Spiritualist 168
The Curse 178
Angels 191

For all early Americans.

CHAPTER ONE

The House on Kestrel Court

"Just hear me out," Sue urged Ellen and Tanya from across the table in a booth at Panera Bread. The aroma of freshly baked pastries filled the air. "And try to keep an open mind."

Ellen sat up in her seat. There was no knowing what crazy idea Sue had cooked up this time. Although it hadn't even been four months since their visit to La Push, and the ghost of Dan Pullen continued to haunt Ellen's dreams, she was always up for a new adventure.

"What's this about, Sue?" Tanya tore off the end of her baguette and dipped it into her potato soup. "I thought we were going to plan our holiday trip to Williamsburg."

"Well, in a way, that's what this is." Sue pushed her dark bangs from her eyes. "I looked up the rental house my mother always stayed in, like I said I would, and I was disappointed to learn that the woman who owned it passed away recently, so the house is no longer available."

"That's no problem." Ellen sat back in her seat. The news was disappointing. Sue had really talked up the house, including the possibility of a haunting. Ellen had been looking forward to another investigation. "I'm sure there are plenty of places to stay in the area."

"There are, there are." Sue nodded before slurping a spoonful of her cheddar broccoli soup. "But this house was so perfect. It sits on a cul-de-sac in a nice residential area and backs up to the woods. It's private and far enough away from the busy touristy areas but close enough to make visiting all the places easy. And this house would have been a nice size for the three of us, with three bedrooms, two and a half baths, and 2500 square feet. It really is the perfect getaway vacation rental."

"I know you wanted to walk in your mother's footsteps." Tanya removed the scrunchie from her blonde ponytail, made the tail tighter, and refastened the scrunchie. "But I'm sure we can find something comparable; don't you think? If we don't wait too late to book it?"

As Ellen took another bite of her Caesar salad, she wondered if that last comment was a jab at her for forgetting to make the reservations for Tanya's birthday trip to La Push back in May.

"So, here's the thing," Sue began. "The house is for sale at a surprisingly low price, considering what houses are going for today. I can't imagine why it's priced so low. So, I was thinking . . . my house at Blackfeet Nation was a great investment as a vacation rental. Maybe Tom and I should do the same thing with this house. The three of us could stay there when we go in December."

Ellen's mouth dropped open. "Really? How exciting."

"Why don't we fly out and take a look at it?" Tanya suggested.

Sue beamed. "I was going to suggest that very thing. Ellen? You in?"

Ellen loved looking at properties, imagining their potential, and fixing them up. "The house is haunted, right? Isn't that what your mother said?"

"She said a creeper followed her everywhere she went," Sue clarified. "She never said whether he originated at the house, or if he caught up to her around town. Honestly, though, I wouldn't mind taking along our gear to investigate."

"I would definitely recommend doing that before committing to a purchase," Tanya advised.

"Sounds fun to me," Ellen said enthusiastically. "When do we leave?"

A week later, on a Thursday afternoon in mid-September, after a morning flight from San Antonio with a layover in Charlottesville, Ellen and her friends sat in their rental car in the driveway of the house on Kestrel Court in Williamsburg, Virginia waiting for the realtor to arrive.

"I'm excited that we get to try it out for a couple of days," Ellen said. "I didn't know such a thing could be arranged."

"Apparently, the seller is eager to unload it," Sue explained.

"The outside of the home is charming," Tanya noted from the passenger's seat.

Sue cut the engine. "I think so, too. I love the three dormers over the garage and the one over the front door. It gives the house a colonial feel, don't you think?"

"Yes, I do." Ellen leaned forward in the back seat. "I'd change out that light fixture over those garage doors—maybe get one with a black iron finish to contrast with the cream-colored siding. It would go nicely with those black shutters."

"That would be pretty," Sue agreed. "And it would look pretty with the brick skirting, too."

Tanya glanced back at Ellen. "It's very similar to Nora Phillips' house, isn't it?"

Nora was the great-granddaughter of Dan Pullen, the ghost who'd haunted the enchanted bungalow in La Push.

"Not really." Ellen cocked her head to the side.

"Like hers, it has the two-door garage on the right," Tanya pointed out. "But instead of being cut into a hillside, this one has steps leading up to the front door. And I bet there are windows on the left near the ground leading to the basement, just like Nora's, too."

Sue turned at the sound of a car approaching. "I guess we're about to find out."

The friends filed out of the vehicle into perfect seventy-degree weather and greeted the young realtor—a black woman who appeared to be in her early thirties. She wore a navy skirt and a flouncy white blouse. Her curly hair fell to her shoulders. Her thin waistline made Ellen wish for the good old days when she had a thin waistline, too.

"Hello," the young woman greeted them. "Which one of you is Sue?"

"That would be me." Sue stepped forward and accepted the woman's outstretched hand. "It's nice to meet you . . . Amanda, right?"

"That's right. So very nice to meet you, too."

"These are my friends, Tanya and Ellen. They're going to help me decide."

Amanda shook hands with them. "So very nice to meet you, ladies. Do you have any questions for me before we go inside and have a look?"

Ellen raised her hand. "Is this house known to be haunted?"

Amanda grinned. "I don't think there's a house in Virginia that isn't haunted. However, I don't know of any stories about this one."

"How far back does the property line go?" Sue wanted to know.

"A half an acre. And there's another half-acre of woods along a green belt behind that. I'll show you once we get to the other side."

Ellen clapped her hands. "I can't wait to see the inside."

"Shall we go in?" Amanda asked.

"Lead the way," Sue replied.

Although there were houses on either side, they were far enough away that the trees and shrubs growing between them gave a sense of privacy from every direction. Even the front porch—made of a pebble-stone aggregate like the seven steps leading up to it—stood far back from the curb. The house was nestled into the trees behind it.

Amanda unlocked and opened the door. "This home was built in the mid-eighties. Homeowners in this area, known as the Seasons Trace community, have access to tennis courts, a basketball court, a swimming pool, and a lot for RV and boat storage. There's also a pond inhabited by fish and ducks with a fountain near the entrance to the community—you may have noticed it driving in."

"Yes, we did," Tanya confirmed.

Ellen followed Sue and Tanya into the house.

"I was hoping for something more colonial," Sue remarked of the interior décor. "This looks like 1990."

Ellen agreed. The blond wood flooring, wallpaper, and wallpaper borders were pretty enough but were dated and certainly not colonial. "We wanted a project, didn't we?"

Tanya opened the closet door. "I don't like this right here in the entryway. It looks like an afterthought."

Tanya was right. Detached from the high ceiling, the closet looked like a box added on to increase the home's storage but not its beauty.

"Ripping that out is the first thing I would do," Ellen agreed. "Losing it would open up the entry."

A set of stairs were built into the left side of the entry, and to the left of the stairs was a cased opening to a formal living room.

"This is nice," Sue said of the living room. "I'd get rid of that wallpaper, of course."

Although a set of blue and pink sofas occupied the room, there was nothing but pink and white striped wallpaper on the walls and a matching window treatment draped over the top of the big front window.

"Most of the sellers' things have already been sold in an estate sale," Amanda explained. "If you see anything left that you'd like to ask for in an offer, just let me know."

"I think I'll pass on those," Sue said of the sofas.

Tanya stopped in her tracks. "I hope we have beds to sleep in."

"Yes, but one of the rooms has an air mattress, because that bed sold."

Ellen touched her finger to her nose. Sue quickly followed suit.

Tanya rolled her eyes. "I guess that's where I'm sleeping tonight."

Attached to the formal living room was a formal dining room with nothing but an outdated chandelier and drapes. Ellen supposed all the furniture from this room had been sold.

"That wallpaper is awful," Ellen said of paper that had been used in the dining room where wainscotting traditionally went. "I'd put wainscotting in its place."

"Absolutely," Tanya chimed in. "Maybe carry it up five feet to picture-rail height, to make it look more colonial."

"I love that idea," Sue agreed. "I wouldn't mind adding some crown molding in here, too."

Across from the dining room was a powder room beneath the stairs, and a cased opening between them led to a kitchen, where the light wood flooring gave way to beige porcelain tile.

Sue stood in the middle of the u-shaped kitchen. "This tile will have to go, too."

"I'd install dark oak throughout this floor," Ellen suggested. "And the kitchen needs a facelift, too."

"I want white, shaker-style cabinets and butcher block countertops," Sue stated. "I've already picked out a backsplash—a simple, subway tile."

"I think black iron handles and light fixtures would go great with that," Ellen said. "I can already see it."

"I like that, too," Tanya agreed.

Amanda led them past a round, glass table and chairs that were tucked in a breakfast nook with a bay window overlooking the woods. From there, they entered a family room with a marble fireplace. The marble was an eighties' terrazzo, which gave the room a dated vibe.

"That needs to go." Sue pointed to the fireplace façade. "We need a craftsman look there. Don't you think? All wood facing."

"Agreed," Tanya said. "But check out these high ceilings and sky lights."

"This is beautiful," Ellen said of the space. "So much natural light."

Even with bare walls and nothing but a blue and white striped sofa, the room was lovely.

To the left of the fireplace, a door led to a sunroom that was built of glass, like a green house.

"This is unexpected," Ellen said, pointing.

"Not to me," Sue confessed. "I've seen the photos on Zillow. Didn't I show them to you?"

A glass door with steps leading down to the ground provided access to the woods.

"I don't recall seeing this sunroom." Ellen gazed out at the woods that dropped along the hillside behind the house. "It feels like a treehouse up here. You're surrounded by woods. This is incredible."

"I wouldn't change a thing in here," Tanya said. "This is where we'll spend all our time."

"Look." Sue pointed to the wall it shared with the family room. "Another fireplace here. It shares the chimney with the one in the next room."

"I'm in love," Ellen exclaimed. "I could see myself snuggled up in here with a good book."

"I could knit in here and drink my hot tea," Tanya imagined.

"Is that a hot tub?" Ellen asked, pointing to what looked like a covered hot tub in the corner.

Amanda grinned. "It is. You ladies might want to try it out tonight."

"I didn't bring a suit," Ellen said. "Did you?"

Sue nodded. "I thought I told you to."

"She told me," Tanya said.

"Is that a deer out there?" Ellen pointed toward the woods. "I saw something move."

"I didn't see it." Sue turned to Amanda. "Do you know if there are deer in this area?"

"Yes, there are," Amanda answered. "And rabbits, squirrels, racoons, and opossums, too."

Sue frowned. "That's not really a selling point for me."

Laughing, Ellen followed Tanya back into the family room and down a hall to the other side of the house into the master suite, where a large wooden sleigh bed and a nightstand were the only furnishings. A beautiful bay window, like the one in the breakfast nook, opened out to the woods behind the house. High ceilings, like those in the family room, added an architectural flare. Although the en-suite bathroom was dated, it was a good size and could easily be refaced. A large walk-in master closet and spacious laundry room over the basement garage completed the first floor.

They followed Amanda upstairs, where a catwalk with views to the family room and entryway below connected the two sides of the house. On one side were two bedrooms and a guest bath, and on the other, the side with the garage, was a large office space. The most attractive feature in the office was a row of three dormers framed with built-in bookshelves.

"I love that," Ellen said of the bookshelves. "This would make an amazing library."

"The carpeting up here looks new," Tanya pointed out. "I wouldn't change it."

Amanda nodded. "It is new. The original owner had it installed just before she passed away. The walls on this floor were recently painted, too."

"She took good care of this place," Ellen noted. "It's in great shape, even for a rental."

"I'm sold," Sue admitted. "I've already made up my mind, and I haven't even seen the basement."

"Well, why don't we go down there, now?" Amanda suggested. "It's unfinished but has a lot of potential."

The basement was accessed through a door on the back of the staircase between the breakfast nook and family room. "Unfinished" was an understatement. The one bulb at the base of the stairs did little to illuminate the dark, musty space, with its exposed wood framing, concrete floor, and shadowy nooks and crannies. The two small windows were covered with cobwebs and offered little in the way of light. When Amanda opened the double garage doors, light flooded in, but even then, cobwebs and shadows dominated the gloomy ambience.

"Who needs a finished basement?" Sue said with a laugh. "I'll never come down here."

"The original owner, Mrs. Glasgow, used to keep it locked and inaccessible to her guests," Amanda reported. "That's why it wasn't kept clean. I don't think she ever came down here either, even though there's plenty of space to park at least two cars."

"You could use it for storage after you rip out that closet upstairs," Tanya suggested.

"That's a good idea," Ellen agreed. "You could put some shelving down here without finishing out the space."

As Ellen walked toward the back wall, a chill ran down her back. There was something eerie about that wall.

"That's strange," she murmured.

"What is?" Sue asked.

"It feels cold and creepy here. I've got chills."

"Maybe that's where Mom's creeper lives," Sue speculated. "Inside that wall."

"What's on the other side of it?" Tanya questioned Amanda.

"There's a storage shed out back. Should we have a look? We can access the backyard through here."

Amanda opened a wooden door that was directly across from the double garage doors. They stepped out to find the glass sunroom above them, forming a covered space on the ground level for an outdoor sitting area. But it was overwhelmed by a storage shed that backed up to the house.

"Is there anything in the shed?" Ellen asked.

"I've left messages with the seller asking for a key, but I don't have one yet," Amanda admitted. "I'm sorry. I don't know what's in there."

Ellen continued to feel something eerie about it. "Maybe *that's* where the creeper lives."

"I feel something emanating from it," Sue admitted. "At least it's down here and not in the main part of the house."

"We can try to talk to him tonight," Tanya pointed out. "Maybe we can help him to move on."

"Are you ghost hunters?" Amanda asked with raised brows.

"Not really hunters," Ellen explained. "More like healers."

"Cool," Amanda said. "If you move to Virginia, you'll have your work cut out for you. We have a lot of ghosts here. Have you visited Colonial Williamsburg? They have ghost tours there, you know."

"We haven't been yet," Sue confessed, "but we plan to go soon."

Amanda pointed toward the woods. "You see where your neighbor's fence ends? Just past these rows of birch trees, where the woods get thick, that's the property line. And like I said, those woods go on for another half-acre."

"I'm glad Mrs. Glasgow never built a fence," Ellen commented. "I love the open view of the woods."

"It's so peaceful," Sue agreed. "I've made up my mind."

Ellen felt another chill on the edge of the woods. Something in the distance moved. It did not look like a deer this time. It looked like a young boy.

"Do children play in these woods?" Ellen asked Amanda. "I thought I saw a boy."

"I suppose it's possible," Amanda admitted. "Though the homes on either side are owned by retirees."

"Maybe grandchildren are visiting," Tanya speculated.

Ellen caught another glance of the boy and gasped. He quickly vanished again, but he'd been there long enough for her to see that he was nearly as transparent as the glass sunroom.

CHAPTER TWO

A Paranormal Investigation

"One glass of wine won't hurt anything," Sue insisted as she climbed into the hot tub later that evening. "It might even make us more relaxed when we try to communicate with the dead."

Although dusk had blanketed the woods, a string of white outdoor lights along the outside of the sunroom emitted a soft glow about a dozen feet out from the house, maintaining the feeling of being up in a treehouse.

Ellen, who wore her bra and panties in the hot tub because she hadn't felt like shopping for a bathing suit, agreed. She took a sip from her wine glass and said, "It's delicious, Tanya. That's all I'm saying."

"I'm fine with my bottled water. You two are going to be dehydrated if you aren't careful."

"Good," Sue jested. "Maybe I'll lose a few pounds of water weight."

"That's not the kind of weight you want to lose," Tanya chastised.

Sue laughed. "I'll take it however I can."

Ellen tried not to envy Tanya's thin form as her friend joined her and Sue in the hot, bubbly water.

"I need to start walking with you again, Tanya," Ellen groaned. "I have twenty pounds that won't stay off—not to mention the other thirty that haven't been off in years."

"You're welcome to join me any time," Tanya said. "Geez, this water's hot."

"It feels good," Sue practically purred.

"Did you ever finish that family tree for Lane and Maya?" Tanya asked Ellen.

"Oh, yeah." Sue sat up. "How's that going? Are the Vanderbilts getting impatient?"

"Not impatient, no. But I think it's hard for families like theirs to understand how families like ours may not know our history as well as they do." Ellen sighed and closed her eyes. "Paul's part of it was easy. And so was my mother's. It's my father's side I can't trace."

"You should try *Twenty-Three and Me*," Tanya suggested.

"I have. I'm still waiting on the results. Meanwhile, I researched the first Frosts. I've learned it's an Anglo-Saxon name from pre-seventh-century Old English."

"I doubt Maya's family expects you to go that far back." Sue said with a laugh.

"Of course not. I just thought if I started way back, I could work my way over to my father's father, who I know absolutely nothing about."

Ellen had never met her paternal grandfather, but she'd imagined him to be funny, like her father. Her dad hadn't been around much while she and Jody were growing up, but he took them fishing a few times without their mother, and he'd shown them a side they'd rarely seen. It was a funny side she had longed to see more often.

"How's that working out for you?" Tanya asked.

"Not great so far. I've read that there were Frosts in England and Scotland. The first to come to America was Thomas Frost in 1635. I found records of early colonists in Michigan, Ohio, New York, and Virginia by the name of Frost, but that's as far as I've gotten."

Ellen put her back against one of the jets, trying to relax her stiff muscles. Researching her family history had brought up a lot of painful memories from her childhood. She was amazed that she and her little brother had survived.

"Well, maybe *Twenty-Three and Me* will come through for you," Sue reassured her.

"So, what do you think of the old man next door?" Tanya, changing the subject, asked. "Can you believe he knew your mother, Sue? How often did she come here?"

"I thought it was only a handful of times," Sue admitted, "but now I think I know why she never invited me to join her."

"She was having a fling with Mr. Benson," Ellen teased.

"It's hard to imagine your mother having a fling,"

"I wasn't imagining *that*. But I am now. Thanks a lot, guys."

Ellen chuckled. "I'm glad she had her bit of fun, if that's what it was."

"Maybe Mr. Benson is the reason she liked Williamsburg so much," Tanya guessed with a grin.

"It's too bad he doesn't know what's in that shed," Sue lamented. "He didn't sound like much of a believer in ghosts, either. In fact, he seemed kind of slow. I'm not sure what my mother saw in him."

Ellen and Tanya laughed.

"What?" Sue bent her brows together.

"He's attractive, even in his eighties," Ellen pointed out. She had barely got her words out when she saw the boy standing on the edge of the woods outside the windows. She sat up and covered her mouth. "There he is again."

"Who?" Tanya turned. "I don't see anyone."

Sue whipped her head around, too. "Me, neither."

"He was right there," Ellen insisted.

Sue cocked her head to the side. "Maybe I was wrong about the wine—at least, in Ellen's case."

"He's gone now, but he was there. It's the same boy I saw earlier." Ellen climbed from the hot tub and wrapped herself in a thick towel. "I'm going to get dressed and start setting up."

Ellen sat at the round, glass table in the breakfast nook across from Sue and Tanya. The flames of three pillar candles in the center of the table danced and cast shadows in the kitchen and on the basement door. Ellen had set up her full-spectrum cameras in the family room and kitchen from different angles. She'd also placed an EVP recorder on the table next to her, along with her EMF reader, digital thermometer, pencil, and notepad. The EMF generator sat on the floor near the hearth and had been turned on before Sue and Tanya had taken their initial readings. All three friends wore their tourmaline rings and *gris gris* bags for added safety. The sage smudge stick they had used to cleanse the house of negative energy lay smoking near the candles in an abalone bowl.

They'd created a circle of protection on the floor around them with salt.

Tanya, who held a pair of noise-cancelling headphones connected to the ghost box app on her phone, asked, "Are we ready?"

Sue nodded. "Put on the blindfold and headphones, and let's make sure you can't hear us."

They had decided to use a method they had learned from Mary Pullen called the Estes Method. Tanya did as Sue requested.

"Tanya?" Ellen tested, once the blindfold and headphones had been put on.

Tanya did not reply.

"Okay." Ellen nodded to Sue. "We're ready."

"Spirits of the other realm, we come in peace," Sue proclaimed. "We mean no harm. We want only to help. If there's anyone here with us, please give us a sign. You can speak to us through this ghost box app by choosing the words you want to say from several radio broadcasts. Or you can give us some other sign. Use the energy from our devices to help."

The room suddenly felt cold.

"Do you feel that?" Ellen questioned Sue.

"Did it get cold to you?"

Ellen nodded. "The thermometer reads sixty-six. That's eight degrees cooler than before."

"Is anyone there?" Sue asked again. "If so, please give us a sign."

"You can use the REM-POD on the kitchen floor," Ellen pointed out. "If you touch it, it will beep."

"Or you could simply knock to let us know you're here," Sue added.

Ellen heard a flutter of noises that sounded like mice in the walls. "Do you think this house has a rodent infestation?"

"Oh, gawd, I hope not," Sue said.

"No," Tanya said abruptly.

Ellen and Sue exchanged looks of confusion.

"No?" Ellen repeated. "We haven't asked you a question yet."

"Us," Tanya said.

"Us?" Sue questioned. "How many of you are there?"

Tanya remained quiet.

"Are there more than two of you?" Ellen asked.

"Thirty-eight, thirty-nine," Tanya counted.

Ellen's brows shot up. Sue's disappeared beneath her bangs.

"Are there thirty-nine spirits in this house?" Sue asked.

"No," Tanya said.

Sue tilted her head to the side. "Are there thirty-nine of you or not?"

"Yes."

Ellen leaned forward and whispered, "Maybe this isn't working. Maybe Tanya isn't answering our questions. What she's saying could be coincidental."

Sue frowned. "Please confirm that there are thirty-nine of you."

"Yes," Tanya said again.

Ellen whispered to Sue, "Maybe there are thirty-nine spirits, but they aren't all in the house?"

"Where are you?" Sue asked.

"Are you in the woods?" Ellen asked. "Are you the boy I saw today?"

"No," Tanya said.

"Don't ask too many questions at once," Sue whispered to Ellen. "We won't know which question is being answered." Then, more loudly, Sue asked, "Are you here in the house with us?"

"Yes."

"I still don't think this is working," Ellen whispered to Sue. "Tanya is just saying yes and no to anything."

The REM-POD on the kitchen floor beeped, causing Ellen to jump in her seat.

"I beg to differ," Sue whispered. Then, more loudly, she asked, "What's your name?"

Tanya didn't say anything for several seconds, so Sue repeated, "Can you tell us something about yourself? Like your name, or how old you were when you died?"

"Lucy," Tanya said.

Sue and Ellen sat up in their seats.

"When did you die, Lucy?" Ellen asked.

"July," Tanya said.

Ellen lifted her brows. "Now we're getting somewhere."

"You died in July?" Sue repeated. "Of what year?"

"Seventy-eight," Tanya said.

"Nineteen-seventy-eight?" Ellen asked.

After a few seconds, Tanya said, "Seventeen."

"Was she seventeen when she died?" Ellen whispered to Sue.

"No," Tanya said.

"Seventeen-seventy-eight?" Sue asked. "Did you die in 1778?"

"Right," Tanya said.

"Revolutionaries?" Ellen whispered.

"Yes," Tanya said.

Ellen sat up straighter in her chair. Now the Estes Method seemed to be working. Were they really speaking with the ghost of an American revolutionary named Lucy who died in 1778?

"Why are you here?" Sue asked.

"Trapped," Tanya said.

"Why?" Ellen asked.

After a few seconds, Tanya said, "Lost."

"How did you die?" Sue asked.

"Evil."

Just then, all three flames of the candles were extinguished, as if someone standing near the table had bent over and blown them out. Ellen noticed the lights on the EMF detector flash from yellow, which showed a low electromagnetic field, to red, which indicated a high one. A high electromagnetic field was often attributed by paranormal investigators to the presence of ghosts, who they believed were comprised of energy.

"Did you blow out our candles?" Sue asked.

"No," Tanya said.

Sue turned to Ellen. "Maybe someone else did."

"Did someone else blow out our candles?" Ellen asked.

"Not . . . me," Tanya said.

"Who?" Ellen asked.

Tanya didn't say anything for many seconds. Then she said, "Evil."

Ellen and Sue exchanged worried looks.

"Is there an evil presence here?" Sue asked.

"Yeah," Tanya said.

"Are you evil?" Ellen asked.

"Friend."

"You want to be our friend?" Sue asked.

Tanya said nothing.

After a minute, Sue asked, "Are you still there?"

Tanya still said nothing.

"If anyone is willing to speak with us, give us a sign," Ellen commanded.

The kitchen light, which had been turned off for the investigation, flickered on and off. The REM-POD beeped twice.

Excitement cursed through Ellen, and she gave Sue a big smile.

"If that was you," Sue began, "please turn the light on and off again."

The light flickered again while the REM-POD remained silent.

"That's incredible," Ellen whispered. "Now I'm convinced."

"I never doubted," Sue said smugly.

"Why are you trapped?" Ellen asked. "How can we help you?"

When nothing happened for many moments, Sue asked, "Can you confirm that there are thirty-nine of you? If so, make that kitchen light flicker twice."

Immediately, the light flickered twice.

"That seems confirmation enough," Ellen whispered. "How can we help these thirty-nine lost souls find peace?"

"Evil," Tanya said again. Tanya pulled off her blindfold and headphones. "Why do I keep saying evil? It's freaking me out."

"I'm not sure," Ellen admitted.

"We think there are thirty-nine souls trapped here, or in the woods behind the house," Sue explained. "They might be American revolutionaries who died in July of 1778. But we don't know about the evil part. We were talking to someone named Lucy."

When another half-hour had passed with no interactions, Ellen and her friends decided to review the footage on the full-spectrum cameras. They each took a camera and synchronized them so they could watch together. Although they picked up the pitter-patter that Ellen had thought sounded like mice in the walls, along with the flashing kitchen light and beeping REM-POD, the cameras hadn't captured anything else that was significant until the candles were extinguished.

"Are you guys seeing that?" Sue asked, unable to take her eyes from her camera monitor.

"The stick man behind you?" Ellen asked.

"I see it, too," Tanya said excitedly. "He bent over the table when the candles went out. Somehow, he blew them out."

"Then he seems to vanish," Ellen observed.

Sue sighed. "We need more data."

"I think they're done talking to us for the night," Ellen said with a shrug.

Tanya stood up. "I'm still freaked out about the evil part, but I'm tired and want to go to bed. Should we sleep in the same room tonight?"

"I could help you drag that air mattress downstairs," Ellen offered, "if you want to sleep in the master with Sue."

"Do you want to share the king with me?" Sue asked Ellen.

Ellen giggled. "That sounds like a line from a renaissance novel."

Sue put her hands on her hips. "What kind of books do you read, Ellen?"

Tanya smirked. "Mystery must be code for reverse harem."

"You'd better sleep in your own bed," Sue teased. "Unless you can keep your sexual proclivities to yourself."

Ellen rolled her eyes. "I guess controlling my urges would be easier than making a second circle of protection."

As the ladies prepared for bed, Ellen asked Sue, "If we can't figure out what the ghosts are trying to tell us, will you still make an offer?"

"Yes. I want to get the ball moving. We'll figure it out eventually. We always do."

"Don't jinx it," Tanya said.

Sue tapped her fist to her head. "Knock on wood."

During the night, Ellen was awakened by a scratching sound—not the scratching of fingernails on skin but of wood against tile. She listened for it again, to be sure she hadn't been dreaming. It came a few seconds later. She sat up in bed.

Not wanting to wake her friends, she quietly opened and closed the circle of protection. Within moments of leaving the circle, she sensed someone standing beside her. She couldn't see anything—not even with her mind's eye—but she could feel a person there with her, too close for comfort.

She left the master bedroom and headed for the living area. The house was dark. Even with the windows uncovered, no light from the moon or stars or streetlamps illuminated the rooms. Ellen fumbled around for a light switch, not recalling where it was. Finally, she found one and flipped it on. The light fixture in the family room turned on and bathed the fireplace and blond floorboards in a soft, yellow light. Ellen didn't notice anything out of place.

Then, she heard the scratching sound again. It was coming from the breakfast nook.

Ellen turned and gasped. The four chairs that had once surrounded the round glass table in the nook had been rearranged. They were now in a row across the kitchen facing into the living area, almost as if to accommodate an audience.

She wondered if the ghost that had followed her from the bedroom was responsible, or if someone else had moved the chairs.

There was another flutter of sounds in the wall, as if mice were chasing each other between the drywalls.

"I'm here to help," Ellen said softly as she crossed the room to pick up one of her full spectrum cameras. "I mean you no harm."

She turned on her camera and made sure that the structured light sensor was enabled and pointed it toward the chairs. Immediately, the screen became filled with humanoid shapes. At least a dozen stick-figures, both adult- and kid-size, could be seen moving around. Four adult shapes sat in the chairs. Smaller figures seemed to be playing on the floor. And still others stood behind the chairs.

Trembling, Ellen said in a shaky voice, "I'm here to help you. I'll find a way to get you to the other side, so you can be at peace."

Just then, she heard water running. On her camera monitor, she observed a tall figure standing in front of the kitchen sink, and one of its arms was moving frantically. Then her camera turned off.

Ellen tried to turn it back on, but the battery was drained. The light fixture overhead flickered. That's when Ellen noticed the writing on the window over the kitchen sink. Afraid to move closer, lest she be surrounded by ghosts, she squinted and leaned forward. When she had finally made out the words, she had a fright. They read: *Get out now!*

"Why do you want me to leave?" she asked gently. "I'm not here to cause you harm."

The light fixture overhead flickered again before going out, and the room was suddenly cold.

With her camera in hand, Ellen scrambled from the room back to the master, where she quickly opened the circle and closed it again. Once she was under the covers, she lay still, listening.

"Ellen?" Sue asked in a sleepy voice. "Everything okay?"

"Yes," she said. "Go back to sleep."

As much as Ellen tried, she never could fall back to sleep. She lay there, listening, until sunlight bathed the room.

CHAPTER THREE

The Second Night

"I can't believe you didn't wake us up," Tanya said, after taking a sip of her coffee where she sat curled in an armchair in the sunroom, still wearing her pajamas.

Ellen, who sat between her friends, had changed the battery in her camera and was showing what she'd captured the previous night.

Sue leaned forward, straining to see the monitor. "I wonder what they're doing," she said of the ghosts appearing as stick-figures.

"I had the sense they were forming an audience," Ellen said. "For what, I have no idea."

"Maybe they entertain each other," Tanya speculated. "And you ruined their show. That's why they wanted you to get out."

"I hope it was as inconsequential as that," Ellen murmured. "But I don't think it was."

Tanya turned to Sue. "Are you still planning to make your offer?"

"Oh, yes. It's already been made. Now, we're waiting to hear back from the seller."

"Why don't we try again tonight?" Ellen said of their investigating. "Maybe we can get some answers that can shed some light on why these spirits can't move on."

Tanya climbed from her chair. "I need to take a shower. What time are we supposed to be at the Kimball Theatre for the walking food tour?"

"Ten o'clock," Sue said. "You still have plenty of time."

Once Tanya had left, Sue turned to Ellen. "Why didn't you wake us up last night?"

"I wanted you to get your sleep. I barely got four hours and not a wink after I recorded this. I don't know how I'm going to manage a three-hour walking tour."

"It's more eating than walking," Sue assured her. "Do you really think I would plan a three-hour *walking* tour? Come on, Ellen. You know me better than that."

Ellen grinned. "Well, *eating* I can handle. I guess I'd better get dressed."

It was another beautiful, clear day in the seventies when Ellen and her friends set out for Colonial Williamsburg in their rental and found a place to park near the Kimball Theatre. They soon found their tour guide—a white woman in her early thirties with short, brown hair and large, black-rimmed spectacles who wore a nametag that read, *Walking Food Tours, April, she/her.*

"Are you here for the walking food tour?" she asked as they approached. "You have your confirmation number?"

"Here you go." Sue handed over her phone with the information.

"Great," April said. "Here are your nametags. I'd appreciate it if you specified your preferred pronouns on the bottom." Then she added, "I'm trying to normalize it, so everyone feels comfortable."

Ellen and her friends followed the guide's directions, and once the rest of their group had arrived—a husband and wife with twin teenaged girls—they started off. Their first stop was the Wythe Candy and Gourmet Shop, where they were given samples of truffles, chocolate-covered almonds, and turtles stuffed with gooey caramel. It was so delicious that Ellen and her friends each bought a box of assorted chocolates.

From there, they walked next door to the Cheese Shop, where every cheese imaginable was there to be sampled. Their hostess also offered them small paper cups of wine to cleanse their pallets after each sample. Ellen and her friends also bought boxes of assorted cheeses.

While they were waiting to pay, Sue's phone rang. After a moment, she hung up and cried, "We got the house!"

Ellen smirked. "Like there was ever any doubt."

"Congratulations," Tanya said. "We'll have to celebrate."

"Let's get stuff for margaritas," Sue suggested. "We can drink them in the hot tub later tonight."

"Great idea!" Ellen said with a grin.

As April led them from the Cheese Shop across Duke of Gloucester Street, she told them about the colonial renewal project in the thirties and forties when Williamsburg, which had once been a thriving community, was seeking ways to rebuild its languishing economy. April told them a bit about the historical buildings—some of which were original, some of which were reconstructed, and most of which were a little of both. While she listened, Ellen felt the hair on the back of her neck stand on end, and goosebumps crawled down her forearms. She also felt a sudden chill in the air and thought she sensed a ghostly presence. Was it the creeper Sue's mom had talked about?

After crossing the street, they stopped at the Spice and Tea Exchange, where they were each given a cup of hot tea with a surprise tea bag.

"Oh, this is delicious," Tanya said after sipping hers. "I taste ginger, nutmeg, and a hint of citrus."

"That does sound good," Sue said. "Mine's minty fresh. It's not my favorite."

"Mine tastes like pomegranates," Ellen said. "It's really good."

Tanya decided to purchase a box of teas before they followed the group to the next stop.

While they walked through Merchant's Square, April told them about the cast of actors and actresses that performed throughout Colonial Williamsburg. Many of them were historians, professional actors, or students at the College of William and Mary. She told them about the great care that went into making their costumes, which the board of trustees required to be historically accurate.

The feeling of a ghostly presence behind Ellen had resumed the moment she'd stepped out of the tea shop. She glanced behind her, and again there was nothing but air.

Ellen turned to Tanya, "Do you sense someone following us?"

"I wasn't going to say anything, but yes."

"I haven't been paying attention," Sue admitted, "but now that you mention it, I think I sense something, too."

"Could it be your mom's creeper?" Tanya wanted to know.

Sue shrugged. "Let's see if we can lose him."

Soon they arrived at the Peanut Shop, where they sampled roasted peanuts with different seasonings, peanut butter, and peanut soup. Before they left, they were each given a peanut-butter cookie.

Next door to the Peanut Shop was the Blue Talon Bistro, where the group was invited to sit at one of two booths to enjoy a small cup of gourmet mac and cheese. It didn't take long for them to gobble up the creamy deliciousness, and then they were on their feet again, headed to the next stop.

Back outside on the street, Ellen sensed the creeper behind her again. She kept glancing back, because it felt like a living person was right on her heels, but no one visible was there.

They followed April across Prince George Street to Kilwins, where they were each given three different samples of fudge. Ellen loved both the mint chocolate and the almond fudge, so she bought some of both. Sue bought some caramel fudge. Tanya chose the vanilla.

Outside of Kilwins, Sue pointed. "Look! It's Aromas Coffeehouse." To April, she asked, "Can we stop in there and get a specialty coffee?"

"Of course," April said. "Be my guest." To the young family, April asked, "Would you like to grab a coffee as well, or should we wait for them at the next stop on the corner?"

"We'll grab coffee, too," the wife and mother replied.

Once inside, Ellen and her friends decided to buy a box of pastries, too.

"What are we going to do with all this food?" Tanya wondered as they left with their coffees and boxes of pastries.

"I'm sure we'll think of something," Sue said with a laugh.

After stopping at the corner for a sample of sweet, iced tea, the group walked up Prince George Street for two blocks before turning west onto Scotland Street. They went another two blocks before April led them inside Paul's Deli, where they each had a slice of made-from-scratch pizza. The crust melted in Ellen's mouth, and the sauce to cheese ratio was perfect. From there, they stepped in next door at Green Leafe Café for beer tasting—all handcrafted beers. Ellen wished Brian were there because beers were his thing. He had breweries all over the west coast.

The combination of wines and beers had Ellen feeling a light buzz as they crossed the street to their final stop, College Delly, where they were each given a four-inch "Hot Holly" sub sandwich, consisting of roast beef, turkey, bacon, American cheese, lettuce, tomato, spicy mayo, and pickles. The bun and veggies were fresh, and the meats were tasty.

"This was one of my favorite walking tours," Sue said as they sat together eating. "Didn't you think it was fun?"

"Like you said," Ellen began, "it was more eating than walking, so, yes, I enjoyed it."

"Me, too," Tanya agreed. "But I still don't know what we're going to do with all this food."

"We'll use it tonight to attract the spirits," Sue suggested. "And maybe we can find out who's been following us all day."

"I think we need to try a different method," Ellen said. "Something other than the Estes Method. We can ask the same questions and see if we get the same answers."

"I like that idea," Tanya said. "That's very scientific of you, Ellen."

"I've been known to have one or two good ideas," Ellen said with a grin.

"I wouldn't go that far," Sue teased.

That evening, they shared a pitcher of frozen margaritas in the hot tub and watched the sun set behind the woods at the back of the house, where the orange and pink hues seeped through the leaves of the trees. Although they hadn't managed to shake off the creeper that had been following them all day, he had seemed harmless so far.

Once night had fallen, Ellen asked, "Well, ladies, should we get to work?"

"Yes," Sue said, as she climbed from the hot tub. "I'm turning into a prune."

The friends went to their respective rooms to change into their pajamas and then reconvened at the breakfast nook, to begin another paranormal investigation of the house.

"I want to try using the dousing rods," Ellen announced. "I've always had good luck with them. And I had another idea. Let's apply the Estes Method to the dousing rods, to take out the human factor. You know what I mean? Sometimes I worry when I'm using them that I'm subconsciously moving them. But if I'm deprived of sight and sound, then the answers are more likely to be legitimate."

"Let's try it," Sue agreed. "Will you be the one going under?"

"I was kind of hoping to ask the questions," Ellen admitted. "Tanya, would you mind?"

Tanya shrugged. "No, I don't mind."

Ellen handed her the headphones. "Just plug them into your favorite playlist."

Tanya did as Ellen had suggested. Then she took the dousing rods before putting on the blindfold.

"Tanya? Can you hear us?" Sue asked.

"Wait," Tanya said. "Let me get my music on."

Tanya took off the blindfold, tapped on her phone, and then put the blindfold back in place. "I'm ready."

"Can you hear us?" Ellen asked Tanya, just to be sure.

Tanya didn't reply.

Ellen leaned over and repositioned Tanya's hands so that the dousing rods were straight. The rods kept moving, so Ellen pulled off Tanya's headphones and said, "Keep your elbows resting on the table and hold your hands against your chest, to keep them steady."

Tanya repositioned herself. "Like this?"

"That's better," Sue said.

"I'll put your headphones on," Ellen said to Tanya. "Don't move."

Once the headphones were back in place, Ellen steadied the dousing rods again.

"Are we ready?" Sue asked her.

Satisfied that the rods had stopped moving, Ellen nodded. "Spirits of the other realm, we come in peace. We mean to help. We want to communicate with you to find out how we can help you to find your way. Feel free to draw energy from our candles and our electronic devices, or from the electricity in this house. Follow the aroma of our food and the light of the candles to find your way to us."

The flutter of mice running through the walls made Ellen jump in her seat.

"We want to ask you some yes or no questions," Sue said. "To answer yes, please move the rod tips away from each other. To answer no, cross the rod tips together. If you don't know the answer, then point them forward, parallel to one another as they are now."

"Is anyone here with us?" Ellen asked.

The rod tips spread as wide apart as they could go.

"That was fast," Sue whispered.

The tips moved back to nearly parallel, though they wobbled a bit.

Once the tops were steady again, Ellen asked, "Is someone named Lucy here with us?"

Immediately, the tips flew apart.

"That seems pretty conclusive," Sue noted.

"I think we need to test this more," Ellen whispered. Then, aloud, she said, "Lucy, is it true that you died in January of 1981?"

The rod tips flew together, crossing slightly.

"Did you die in July of 1778?" Sue asked.

The rod tips flew apart.

Ellen and Sue exchanged nods.

"Are you the only spirit in this house?" Ellen asked.

The rod tips flew together.

"Are there really thirty-nine of you haunting this area?" Sue asked.

The rod tips wobbled a bit but remained parallel.

"Do you know how many are haunting this house?" Ellen asked.

The rod tips flew apart.

"Hmm." Sue frowned. Then she asked, "Are there thirty-eight of you?"

The rod tips wobbled toward each other but then flew apart again.

"So, there's thirty-eight, not thirty-nine of them," Ellen whispered.

The rod tips remained apart.

"Were you American revolutionaries?" Sue asked.

The tips wobbled a bit and then flew apart again.

"Did you die in a battle?" Ellen asked.

The rod tips swung together.

"Illness?" Sue asked.

The rod tips separated but then crossed again at the tips.

"Did you die an accidental death?" Ellen asked.

The rod tops remained crossed.

"Did someone kill you?" Sue asked.

The rod tips flew apart. At that moment, the candles went out, and a temperature drop chilled the house.

Tanya removed her blindfold and headphones. "It got cold all of a sudden. What's going on?"

Ellen felt as if whatever had been following them was standing just behind her. She took up the dousing rods, steadied her arms and hands until the rods were parallel, and asked, "Lucy, are you the one who was following us today in Williamsburg?"

The rod tips crossed.

"Do you know who was following us?"

The rod tips flew apart.

Ellen sighed, wishing she could ask for a name. "Why don't we try another method that allows for more than yes or no questions?"

"Our only choices are the Ouija Board and the ghost box app," Sue pointed out.

"I don't want to go under again," Tanya said. "I've got the creeps. I think that creeper from today followed us home."

Ellen put down the dousing rods and took out her phone. "Let's just use the app without anyone going under. We can review everything on the cameras, to see if what we hear in the moment matches with what we catch on the cameras.

"Sounds good," Sue said. "I'll start." She cleared her throat. "Spirits of the other realm, thank you for speaking with us tonight. We have another device we'd like to try. It shuffles through radio broadcasts. You can channel your energy into selecting the words you'd like to use to answer our questions."

"Leave," a voice on the app said over Ellen's phone.

"Why do you want us to go?" Sue asked.

"Evil."

Tanya shot a worried glance at Ellen and Sue. "Not again."

"Leave," the voice came again. "Now."

Ellen jumped to her feet. "What should we do? This message seems pretty clear. They don't want us here."

Tanya stood up, too. "Maybe we should get a hotel for the night."

"I'm buying this house," Sue said aloud. "I'm not leaving."

"Run," the voice said over the app. "Evil . . . run."

"Are you evil?" Sue asked.

"The . . . hair."

"Did that say *hair*?" Tanya asked. "That doesn't make sense. Maybe that thing doesn't really work one hundred percent of the time."

"Maybe not," Ellen said. "Maybe we're getting worked up for nothing."

"Let's review what we've recorded," Sue suggested. "Maybe the cameras caught something that we didn't."

As they reviewed their footage, Ellen continued to sense a foreboding presence watching over her shoulder.

"Look there." Tanya showed them her monitor, where a stick person was standing near their table. "It keeps touching the dousing rods."

Sue's brows shot up. "That must be Lucy."

"Oh my gosh," Ellen said when a second figure appeared behind her on the monitor. It put its hand on her shoulder and just stood there, touching her. "I hope that isn't the evil thing Lucy seems to be warning us about."

"While I believe the ghost app gives us valuable data, I'm not sure it can always be trusted," Tanya remarked. "I think we'd know if we were in the presence of something evil. Don't you?"

"I think so, too," Sue said. "And I don't sense it. Anyway, I'm not backing down—not now that my offer has been accepted."

Ellen wanted to agree with them about the ghost box app sometimes being wrong, but the eerie feeling of someone not of this world standing close behind her continued to haunt her, even as they readied for bed.

CHAPTER FOUR

The Shed

"This lobster fettucine is amazing," Tanya exclaimed at the table at the Fat Canary, where she sat between her husband, Dave, and Ellen's husband, Brian.

"It can't be as good as my duck," Dave teased before taking another bite.

"All the travel sites highly recommended this place." Sue cracked open a lobster tail. "I'm glad we were able to get dinner reservations."

It was a little loud down in the crowded basement of the bar and restaurant near Colonial Williamsburg, but the food and wine were worth the extra effort of having to speak over the noise. Not a fan of lobster, Ellen enjoyed her grilled salmon—though, she had to admit that after tasting Brian's beef tenderloin, she wished she had gotten that instead. Ellen's little black dog, Moseby, who was curled on her lap in his cloth pooch carrier, seemed to prefer the salmon.

Brian raised his glass of red wine in the air. "A toast to the new homeowners."

Sue scoffed "Honeymooners?"

"*Homeowners*," Tom corrected.

Sue laughed. "Oh. That makes more sense. Brian and Ellen are the only newlyweds around here."

"Not really newlyweds anymore." Ellen smiled at Brian.

Tom clinked his glass against Sue's before tapping it to the other glasses. "Cheers."

"Cheers," everyone else echoed.

Brian lifted his chin. "You know, Sue, you don't have to be newlyweds to be honeymooners."

Sue chuckled before glancing at Tom. "Thank you, Brian. I'll take that under advisement."

Ellen and Tanya giggled. The men shook their heads.

Sue put a hand on Tom's shoulder. "I know I tease him all the time, but, honestly, I didn't know what happiness was until I married him."

"And by then it was too late," Dave said with a laugh.

Ellen threw her head back and guffawed.

Sue and Tom had closed on the house on Kestrel Court that morning—only two weeks after Ellen and her friends had viewed it. After the signing, Sue and Tom had joined Ellen and Tanya and their husbands—and Moseby—for a tour of historical Jamestown before taking the ferry to Surry. It had been a beautiful day in early October with temperatures in the low sixties—not cool enough for a jacket, unless you were Tanya. After some light shopping, they'd returned to the mainland and toured historical Yorktown before lunching at Yorktown Pub, overlooking Yorktown Beach. Despite the beautiful October day, Ellen and her friends and their spouses had been the only people strolling along the shoreline beside gentle waves and beneath squawking gulls. It had been the highlight of Moseby's day, even if it hadn't been a large beach.

From there, the group had toured Colonial Williamsburg. Ellen had been fascinated by the history behind the town and its buildings, especially that of the beautiful Governor's Palace, where she and Brian had walked Mo along the grounds and had taken photos for the kids. Although Ellen had enjoyed her sight-seeing immensely, she had been unable to shake the feeling that the Virginia creeper had been following them throughout the day.

One of the colonial homes that had felt particularly oppressive had been the Peyton Randolph House—second in size only to the Governor's Palace. The tour guide had given them quite an education on colonial architecture and the lifestyle of the early American revolutionaries, but Ellen had gotten the feeling that there was more to the house than the guide was telling them.

"I'm dying to see what's in that shed," Ellen said, once she'd finished her salmon.

"Tom packed his bolt cutters for that very purpose," Sue assured her. "Right, Tom?"

"Oh, yeah. That tool can penetrate just about anything."

Dave leaned forward in his chair. "That's what she said."

Tanya turned pink and rolled her eyes.

Back on Kestrel Court, Ellen stood beside Brian, with Moseby on his leash, on the edge of the woods behind the house while Tom put his bolt cutters to use. Brian held a light. Moseby whined and paced about nervously, which only added to Ellen's uneasiness. Ellen was beginning to think that this was something they should have tried in the light of day. There was no telling what might happen when those old doors were finally opened. The creepiness surrounding the shed had her on edge.

"It's okay, Moseby-Mo," Ellen cooed.

When Tom failed to break the lock, Dave took over, but even he had no luck. Brian couldn't resist giving it a go, too, even though success was doubtful.

"Oh, darn." Ellen couldn't hide her disappointment when Brian couldn't break the lock, either. "What do we do now?"

"So much for your tool being able to penetrate just about anything," Sue said to Tom with a wry grin.

Ellen and Tanya giggled. Tom shook his head.

"It's too bad the hinges are on the inside," Dave pointed out. "Otherwise, we could have removed the doors."

"Or the hardware holding the padlock," Tom added. "We can't unscrew the latches because they're sandwiched in between the layers of the doors."

Brian put an arm around Ellen. "I'll ask the contractor to bust it open in the morning. He'll know what to do."

"That's a good idea." Ellen gave Brian a smile. "Let's go inside. I don't like the vibe out here at night."

While the men enjoyed the hot tub, Ellen and her friends set up their equipment to conduct another paranormal investigation, hoping to get to the bottom of who the thirty-eight or thirty-nine souls were and why they were trapped.

"I made some progress on my family tree," Ellen announced to her friends while she lit the candles on the table. "It turns out that I'm related to a family of Frosts in Richmond. I've reached out to them through the *Twenty-Three and Me* app to see if any of them know anything about my father's family."

"That's great," Tanya said. "Richmond is so close to here. Maybe you can arrange to meet some of them in person."

"Maybe so." Ellen smiled. She sometimes felt as if she and her brother were the only Frosts left—aside from their children. Both of their parents had been the only child in their families, so they had no aunts and uncles or cousins. It was a strange feeling not having older relations. It highlighted the fact that she was the next in the family line to die.

Sitting at the round, glass table with their three candles lit, Sue, who had agreed to wear the blindfold and headphones this time, announced, "I'm ready when y'all are."

"You can't hear us?" Ellen tested.

Sue sat waiting and did not reply.

Ellen glanced at Tanya, who said, "Go ahead."

Ellen took a deep breath. "Spirits of the other realm, we come in peace. We mean you no harm. We're here to help. If anyone is here with us tonight, can you give us a sign? You can draw energy from our devices."

Ellen mentioned the EMF generator, the REM-POD, and the ghost app that shuffled various radio broadcasts. Then she added, "You could also knock, turn on a light, or indicate your presence in some other way."

"I'm serious!" Dave's voice carried from the sunroom. "Tanya! Come here! Ladies?"

Ellen and Tanya exchanged looks, and then tapped Sue's shoulder.

"The men are calling us," Tanya explained after Sue had removed the headphones and blindfold.

The three women rushed from the breakfast nook to the sunroom to see what the men wanted.

"Did something happen?" Sue asked.

"Yes." Dave stood in the hot tub holding his chest. "Something pushed me under and held me down. They don't believe me, but it's true."

Brian and Tom laughed.

"Dave, this is serious," Tanya insisted. "Quit playing games."

"I'm not. I know this is serious. Why won't you believe me?"

"I believe him," Ellen said. "Look at his hands. He's shaking."

Tanya grabbed one of the towels and helped Dave from the tub. "I'm sorry. It's just that you're always the jokester."

"I know. I understand. But I'm being serious right now. I thought I was going to drown. Those jackasses thought I was playing, too."

Brian made an "ouch" with his mouth to Ellen, who shrugged.

"Sorry, man," Tom apologized. "You were taunting the ghosts just before you went under. I thought you were pranking us."

Ellen sighed "I'm glad you're okay. Why don't you guys dry off and get dressed while we finish up?"

"Not a bad idea," Brian agreed. "We still need to carry that air mattress upstairs."

When Ellen returned to the breakfast nook, she noticed the water at the kitchen sink was running. She could tell it was hot water because steam was rising from the basin.

"Guys, look at this." She turned off the water.

In the condensation on the window, words had been written in all caps.

Sue read, "The *something* buyer beware?"

"The *home* buyer?" Tanya guessed.

The second word had been written in an area with less condensation and wasn't legible.

"Great," Sue groaned. "Now I've got chills."

When the men entered to see what the women were talking about, Sue said, "Tom, I hope you can sleep with your eyes open."

"I don't think they'll be closing much after this," he admitted.

"Would you ladies prefer to get a hotel for the night?" Brian offered.

Although Ellen had shared stories with Brian about her paranormal investigations, he'd rarely experienced them himself. He only had a hint of what she and her friends had endured and the bravery they'd needed to do it.

"I think we're okay to stay." Ellen turned to her friends. "What do you think?"

"We always have our circles of protection," Sue pointed out. "We'll be okay, I think."

Tanya nodded her agreement, but the men looked less convinced.

While their spouses went to dry off and change, the women tried again to speak with spirits, but nothing more happened. Even while they reviewed the camera footage, hoping to see the stick figure again, they caught nothing. Although one of the cameras had been pointing into the kitchen, the sink was far off in the shot—too far to catch the sink faucet turning on. The steam was apparent, but not the writing of the words on the window.

Disappointed with their findings, the three friends readied for bed, each making circles of protection around them and their husbands. Ellen suspected that if the men had been skeptical about the need for salt, they weren't anymore.

Brian wrapped an arm around Ellen and kissed her goodnight. Moseby lay curled up between them. Ellen hoped her circle of protection would hold against whatever evil they'd been warned about.

The next morning, Ellen was relieved to learn that nothing unusual had happened to anyone during the night. No one had slept well, having been unnerved by the ghostly threat on Dave's life and the warning on the window. Brian made pancakes and sausage while Ellen took Moseby for a walk in the woods, which were less creepy in the daytime, even beneath the light sprinkling of rainfall. She was hoping to see the boy again. Maybe he would talk to her and answer some of her questions. But, after twenty minutes, he never showed, so Ellen returned with Moseby indoors.

The contractor whom Brian had recommended to Sue and Tom arrived at nine o'clock with two assistants to hear Sue's plans and to provide an estimate. They went from room to room, while Sue, Ellen, and Tanya shared their ideas. At the end of the tour, the contractor and his team promised they could finish the job in seven weeks.

"Perfect." Sue beamed. "That should give us plenty of time in December to come for a holiday visit."

"We want to go to Busch Gardens," Ellen explained to the contractor and his men. "We're told it's the most Christmassy place in America."

"That's a fact," Jason, the lead contractor, affirmed. "It's a great place. My wife and kids go a few times a year."

"*You* don't?" Tom asked with a wry grin.

Jason shrugged. "It's not really my thing. I do a lot of manual labor, and the last thing I want to do on my day off is walk around."

"I get it," Tom said.

Sue scoffed. "What? You wouldn't know manual labor if it hit you in the face."

Tom rolled his eyes and said to the other men, "See what I mean?"

The men laughed, which chastened Sue, who said, "He knows I'm only kidding. Though, if you ever watched him peel a carrot, you'd know what I mean."

"You don't have to be good in the kitchen to know manual labor," Dave said on Tom's behalf. "Tanya can't cook worth beans, but you should see her other manual labor, if you know what I mean."

Dave made a crude gesture.

Tanya elbowed him in his gut and cried, "Dave!"

"I'm talking about pulling weeds," he said defensively—though he winked at Brian. "She's especially fastidious when it comes to pulling weeds in the garden."

"Well, that's true," Tanya said, her face still as red as a beet. "But my cooking's not that bad."

Dave squeezed Tanya's shoulders. "Well, let's just say your weeding is better."

Jason cleared his throat. "Why don't you show me that shed you need opened?"

"This way." Brian led the way down to the basement.

A few minutes later, the group gathered outside where the sprinkling had stopped to watch Jason have his try with bolt cutters. He thought that maybe Tom's hadn't been sharp enough, but after several attempts from him and his two companions, they gave up on that method. Then Jason took a couple of nut wrenches, placed them in the hook of the lock, and pushed the wrenches together, hoping to bust it open. He tried this for at least five minutes before giving up on that method, too. Next, he cut an aluminum Coke can into strips and created shims, which he used to try to shimmy the lock free from the locking mechanism. Ellen and her friends went inside after watching for twenty minutes, and the men kept at it for over an hour before giving up on that method, too,

Dave texted Tanya: *You ladies might want to see this.*

Tanya read the text to her friends. They went downstairs and out back to see what was going on.

"We've tried every method we know to attempt to open or break the lock without damaging the shed," Jason explained. "So now we're going to use a chainsaw to cut down the doors."

"Stand back," Brian warned the group.

Everyone took a few paces back. Mo began to whine, so Ellen picked him up and held him in her arms.

Once the doors were down, the onlookers had a shock: the shed was empty.

"Why would someone go through the trouble to padlock an empty shed?" Tom wondered.

"Look in here." Jason motioned to Tom to join him inside. "It's a trap door."

Ellen, Sue, and Tanya gawked at one another.

Jason opened the door. "Shall we go down?"

CHAPTER FIVE

A Secret Crypt

Using the lights on their phones to see by, Tom, Brian, and Ellen followed Jason down the stone steps into an old cellar. Only about fifteen feet by fifteen feet, it had a concrete floor, brick walls, and four old steel footings holding a foundation overhead that Jason said had once held up a house.

"What in the world?" Tom pointed to something in one of the corners.

Ellen shined her light in that direction and gasped. It was a pile of what appeared to be human bones.

"Could these be your ghosts?" Brian asked.

"I would bet my life on it," Ellen replied. "I wonder why they were discarded in this way."

"I think these might help." Tom was bent over one of four old trunks that were pushed up against the brick wall. "Take a look."

Ellen and Brian moved to either side of Tom and shined their lights inside the dusty, wooden crate. Something slithered past Ellen's foot. She shrieked and did a series of knee lifts.

"It's just a bull snake," Jason said. "It's harmless."

"It's huge," Ellen protested, panting.

The brown and white spotted creature was at least six feet long. It curled up in a corner, as far away from the humans as possible.

"Nonvenomous, though," Jason assured her.

"You alright?" Brian asked Ellen.

Ellen gave him a nod, though her heart was still racing. This cellar was cold and creepy, and she was picking up all kinds of eerie vibes.

"What's going on down there?" Tanya asked from above. "Do you see anything?"

"I just saw a snake," Ellen warned. "And there's a pile of skeletons down here."

"Seriously?" Tanya asked.

"Take photos!" Sue shouted.

Ellen made her way back to Tom's side and peered into the chest before taking a few photos.

"A handkerchief just disintegrated in my hand," Brian said, "so be careful."

"These papers are holding up," Tom said. "They look like letters."

Brian pointed his light at a stack of books. "That's an old Bible."

Tom opened another one of the trunks. "This one's empty except for what looks like a snuff box."

Brian opened another. "This one's empty, too."

"What's in this one?" Jason wondered as he lifted the lid to the last trunk. "It's another Bible and a pair of broken spectacles, but, otherwise, it's empty, too. I think those victims were robbed of anything valuable."

"Can you guys carry this one up the steps?" Ellen asked of the trunk that was full of papers and books.

"Let me help you with that," Jason offered as he changed places with Ellen.

Trying to shake off the suffocating, eerie energy stifling her in the cellar, Ellen took a few photos of the bones in the corner and then, keeping one eye on the snake, shined her light around the room to take a more careful look at the space while the men carried the chest upstairs. Had Mrs. Glasgow, the last owner of the house, known about this cellar? Is she the one who'd put the lock on the doors of the shed, or had she inherited the shed and had been unable to open the padlock?

Ellen gathered the broken spectacles, Bible, and snuff box and then found her way back to the stone steps, not wanting to be left alone down there for a second longer. As she ascended the stairs, she decided she would call her friend, the anthropologist Bob Brooks, from the University of Oklahoma. Maybe he could tell them something about the bones.

"We'd better carry this inside," Tom advised once they were out of the cellar. "We don't want it further damaged by the elements."

It had begun to sprinkle again.

"What is it?" Sue asked as she followed the group back into the basement.

"We don't know yet," Ellen confessed, "but we suspect whatever's inside that trunk may have belonged to the bodies that were lying in a pile beside it."

"How many bodies?" Dave wanted to know as he followed them upstairs.

"It was hard to tell," Brian said. "But I'd say dozens."

"Thirty-eight?" Tanya asked.

Tom shrugged. "It's possible."

Ellen shuddered.

"You might need to notify the local authorities about the human remains," one of Jason's assistants informed them.

"We know an anthropologist who will want to study them first," Ellen replied. "We don't want those bones to end up in an evidence locker before our friend and his team can study them properly."

"We'll eventually report this to the proper authorities," Sue assured him.

"I guess my team and I will leave you to it," Jason said. "We'll be back on Monday to begin demolition."

"I'll leave the key under the mat," Tom offered. "We only have one, or I'd give it to you now."

"Sounds good." Jason and his men made their way to the front door. "I'll keep you posted on the job. And, Sue, if you could get everything ordered and have it delivered here as soon as possible, that will help us stay on track. Have them deliver everything to the back of the house near the back door."

"Will do," Sue promised.

Jason and his crew left, leaving Ellen and her friends to mull over the items in the chest.

Ellen carefully picked up a yellowed envelope. Some of the writing on the outside was legible. It was addressed to a Miss Lucy something in Williamsburg, Virginia.

Ellen gasped. "Oh, my gosh! This one is addressed to Lucy! Maybe it's the Lucy who communicated with us!"

"I've got chills!" Tanya cried. "What does it say?"

Ellen gingerly pulled out the letter, unfolded it, and, finding it surprisingly legible, read aloud:

"'My dearest sister, I have only a moment to dash off a few sentiments to you. The members of our camp are celebrating the glorious news from France, which may have reached your city by this time, offering an alliance from France and Spain with honourable terms. We are confident that this will cause a peace before the leaves (which now are just budding out here) fall from their tinder sprigs. With all my love, Edmund.'"

Ellen added, "The letter is dated May 9, 1778."

"She must have died two months later," Tanya reasoned. "I hope not, but that's how it seems."

"Listen to this one," Sue urged. "It's dated July 23, 1775. It reads, 'Dear Madam, I hope you and the children are well and will continue to be so until I can finally come home to you. I know I said in my last letter that it would be this summer, but the general has given orders that we are not to leave camp and has made no mention of when his mandate will be lifted. I hope you understand that I am obligated to comply with the order.' The next line is too faded to read, but after that, it says, 'Tell our children that Daddy has not forgotten them and that they must continue to study their books. I have sent paper for them to make bonnets. Your ever-loving husband, Sam Cooper.' Below that, he added, 'I part with a kiss.'"

"They sound like letters written home by revolutionary soldiers," Tom pointed out. "I hope those skeletons don't belong to their families."

"I bet they do," Dave speculated.

Ellen had carefully returned the letter from Edmund to its envelope and had taken up another. Before she could read it, Brian held up a book.

"This Bible contains a family tree," he pointed out. "Edmund and Lucy Dickinson are both listed in it."

"Here's another one," Dave said. "It lists a family called Scammel."

A surge of excitement coursed through Ellen. "We have a lot of work ahead of us. How would y'all feel about skipping our plans for today so we can comb through these treasures?"

"I didn't want to go on the ghost tour, anyway," Dave confessed. "And this stuff sounds fascinating."

"This is *your* deal," Brian said to the ladies. "We're just here to look pretty."

"Then Tom better clean up his act," Sue teased.

Everyone chuckled, including Tom.

Brian made more coffee while the rest of them sat down and began reading. Ellen, Tanya, Sue, and Brian sat at the table in the breakfast nook, while Tom and Dave made themselves comfortable on the family room sofas.

"This one's interesting," Dave piped up after a few minutes of silent reading. "A young man by the name of William Barton writes to his parents about his captivity in England after finally being rescued and returned to America. He describes being closely confined in a dirty and cold prison deprived of every necessity of life for two full months. He says to his parents that he thanks God that he remains in a perfect state of health, for many of his fellow prisoners suffered illness and even death."

"I bet those parents were relieved to hear from their son," Sue commented. "But I guess they were the unlucky ones, if they're lying on that heap of bones down there."

"Listen to this," Tom chimed in. "It's a letter written from a soldier named Alexander Scammel in 1775—I can't tell the month, because that part is smudged. He writes, 'Brother Phillips, I urge you to reconsider your stance on service to our great country. Tyranny and oppression wield their iron rod over our young nation, shaking the very foundation of our constitution and the work of our founding fathers. I can hear their voices from the ground below my feet, crying out for us to remember the rights, liberties, and this land itself, which they so dearly purchased. I understand your desire to fight at home—to protect your wife, young children, and ailing parents. I believe you when you tell me the dangers you have faced while protecting and defending your community. And the stories you have told me about the Indians attacking our cities on behalf of the British I have heard from other sources. But any man of true honor and virtue would be here, at camp, because here we fight the real enemy of freedom.'"

"I don't think I like his attitude," Tanya admitted.

"I doubt Brother Phillips did either," Sue guessed.

"The letter I'm reading describes a similar difficulty for the Americans at home," Tanya began. "This one soldier writes in 1777 to his wife and four young children, saying how distressed he is to hear of the dangers his family endured in his absence. He says that although he is away at camp, they are as much revolutionary war soldiers as he. He asks his young sons and daughter to be brave for their mother the next time the Indians come to harass their town on behalf of the British. He says he wants to see them very much, and though they are separated by a great distance, his heart is with them. He writes that he and the other soldiers will be marching soon to another location but where, they do not know. He says that some say New York. He adds that lately the only thing he can think of are his wife's pickles and cold meat, which he misses almost as much as he misses his family."

"I like what he said about the American settlers at home being revolutionary soldiers, too," Ellen stated. "Sometimes we forget what the families at home endured. I hope we can piece together what happened to those people in the cellar."

Brian lifted a yellowed page in his hand. "This is a sad stack of letters to the parents of a soldier. The first three letters are from the son, a Lieutenant Gregory Smith. The first is dated November 22, 1777, and he describes how surprised he is to not have been given any leave by now to come home. He seems to have no idea of what he signed up for, but says that people are resigning left and right, so maybe there will be a promotion in it for him if he stays."

"Sounds reasonable," Dave said with a shrug.

"The second letter," Brian continued, "dated February 18, 1778, reiterates his belief that he should be home on leave, and he says that all hopes of doing so before April have been blasted. He also asks his parents to write, saying he 'should glad of a few lines if convenient, and perhaps a few pounds of sugar and a little chocolate, which are scarce at camp these days.'"

"He sounds young," Tom noted.

Sue nodded. "I bet he was. Maybe he was Luke's age."

"Or younger," Tom speculated.

"He certainly sounds young in the third letter, dated March 2, 1778," Brian said. "He thanks his parents for the sugar, chocolate, and shirts and stresses how much he needed the shirts and how bad the conditions are and how he longs to be home with them. He says the camp life doesn't agree with him, and he's seen so many of his friends killed, that he prays to God it will all be over soon."

Ellen shuddered. "I can't imagine what it must have been like for those parents. Can you imagine Nolan or Lane at a military camp, and us having to read letters of how scared and distressed they are?"

"It's unfathomable," Brian agreed. "But a lot of parents go through this even today."

Dave, who had crossed the room to the kitchen to pour another cup of coffee, added, "True. It's a hard fact of life."

"So, what does that final letter say?" Sue wanted to know.

"It's written by his friend, another lieutenant by the name of Robert Goodwin, and it's dated March 31, 1778. The friend writes to inform the parents that their son was wounded in battle and is very unwell with no hope of improving. He writes that the son is too injured to tolerate horseback, so he writes on the son's behalf asking the parents to please send a wagon for him. The son does not wish to spend his remaining days at camp."

Tears filled Ellen's eyes. "I'm so grateful that we haven't had to endure that kind of pain."

Brian squeezed her hand.

In the next instant, a cold shiver worked down Ellen's spine. She felt a cold hand on her shoulder, though she knew no one living was standing behind her.

"Ellen?" Sue leaned across the table. "Are you okay? You suddenly don't look well."

Ellen held her breath for several seconds. She felt a squeeze on her shoulder, and then the sensation of being touched ended as abruptly as it had begun.

"Babe?" Brian asked, taking her hand again. "What's the matter?"

"Someone touched my shoulder," she whispered. "It felt as real as your hand."

Tanya straightened her back. "I bet it was one of the parents addressed in those letters!"

"That makes sense," Sue agreed.

"What will you ladies do to help these lost souls?" Dave asked from the kitchen, where he sipped his coffee. "*Can* you help them?"

"We can," Sue promised. "And spirits of the other realm, if you are listening, know that we are here to help you. We will find a way to help you to cross over to the other side and find the restful peace you deserve."

CHAPTER SIX

Return to Williamsburg

In mid-November, Ellen, Sue, and Tanya returned from San Antonio to the house on Kestrel Court in Williamsburg to meet with the contractor, inspect the progress on the renovations, and continue their investigation into the thirty-eight ghosts haunting the house.

With the help of their anthropologist friend, Bob Brooks, they'd confirmed that the bones in the hidden cellar belonged to men, women, and children who had likely died during the American revolutionary era. Bob and his team had wanted to pack up the remains and transfer them to his lab at the University of Oklahoma, but Ellen and her friends had persuaded him to wait until they had finished their investigation.

"Moving the remains to another location may confuse the tethered spirits even more," Ellen had explained.

Bob had then asked them to allow him and his team to use the basement on Kestrel Court as a makeshift lab, so that they could begin their work without having to relocate the skeletons. Ellen and her friends had agreed, which meant there were two crews at the house—a construction crew renovating the interior, and an anthropology team analyzing bones in the basement. Over the course of a week, Bob and his team had counted thirty-eight bodies and had sealed each set of remains in thick protective plastic. Then they had returned to Oklahoma while they waited for DNA results from samples they had sent to their biomedical lab.

Meanwhile, Ellen and her friends had finished reading the letters and diaries they'd discovered in the cellar trunk. Tanya had created an Excel spreadsheet documenting each artifact. Once they had finished, they sent the materials over to Bob to be studied by him and his team.

Now, they were back in Williamsburg at the house with Jason for a walk-through. In the mid-forties, the weather was chilly enough for coats this time around, which Ellen thought a welcome change from the Texas heat, where forty-degrees was still rare in mid-November.

"This entryway looks so much nicer without that ugly closet," Tanya remarked as she followed Sue inside. "It's so spacious now."

"I agree," Jason said as he took up the rear.

Everything looked so lovely to Ellen that she wasn't sure what to look at first. Then, the new wooden floors caught her eye. "These floors look fabulous."

The old couches had been removed from the formal living room and the family room, making it possible to see the floors from one side of the house to the other.

"I'll tell you what," Sue began, "I just couldn't be happier with the way this is turning out. Look at those kitchen cabinets. Aren't they beautiful?"

"They are," Tanya agreed. "Especially against the wood flooring."

"When will they install the butcher block countertops?" Ellen wanted to know.

"That's one of the last things we do," Jason explained. "We still need to install the backsplash and some of the trim. We also want to get the new appliances in here to make sure the countertops fit just right."

"The wainscotting in the dining room looks perfect," Sue said. "I'm glad we decided to paint it cream, to subtly contrast with the white paint on the walls."

"Yes," Jason agreed. "You wouldn't want it all the same color, and stained wood might have made the room feel too dark."

"The cream was your idea, Jason," Sue recalled, "so thanks for that."

"My pleasure."

Ellen looked at the walls in the family room. "The wall paint in here looks nice, too. Really freshens up the space."

Tanya nodded. "So much better than that wallpaper, which totally dated the home."

"Check out the fireplace!" Sue exclaimed as she pointed to the wooden façade. Unlike the wainscotting, it had been stained a dark oak, to match the wood floors. "It's absolutely gorgeous!"

Jason smiled. "I'm so glad to hear it."

They peeked into the powder room, where everything had been done but the new light fixture, before heading to the master suite. The furniture had been sold, so it was just a blank room with the new wooden flooring and painted walls instead of wallpaper. But it looked completely transformed.

"Check out my bathroom!" Sue cried gleefully. "I love my new tub!"

"That's the only room that's finished," Jason confessed.

"It looks like you're ahead of schedule," Sue observed. "You said seven weeks, and it's only been five, and everything is almost done."

"We'd rather over-estimate than the other way around," Jason conceded. "You never know if an order is going to be late. So far, everything has come in except for the appliances, but those won't take long to install."

Sue lifted her brows. "The butcher block countertops are in?"

"Yes, ma'am. I'm storing them in the basement, along with the backsplash and light fixtures."

"I'm surprised there's room in there with all the dead bodies," Ellen commented.

"In any other scenario," Sue began, "that statement would be incriminating."

"I promise I'm being careful," Jason assured them. "Though, I don't think they've liked us banging around."

"What do you mean?" Sue asked.

"Most of the time, we thought we were imagining things. But enough weird stuff has happened that this house has made believers out of us."

"What kind of weird stuff?" Tanya wanted to know.

"Moving our tools, knocking over things . . . all harmless but unnerving nevertheless."

"I'm glad no one was injured," Sue said with a frown.

"You and me both," Jason said with a laugh.

"Is the bathroom upstairs finished?" Tanya asked as she headed upstairs. "I want to see my room, too."

"All but the light fixtures," Jason replied.

"*Your* room?" Sue echoed. "Does Ellen agree on your choice?"

"Oh, it doesn't matter to me." Ellen flipped a hand through the air as she followed Tanya. "Tanya can pick."

Once they were upstairs, Ellen regretted her words, because the view of the woods from Tanya's room was spectacular. Ellen's room had views of the cul-de-sac and the house next door—though a line of trees provided a semblance of privacy.

It wasn't like she and Tanya would be staying there often, anyway. So, what did it matter?

The upstairs bathroom had finishings similar the master bath and powder room: white cabinets, black granite countertops, and a white marble backsplash. The white marble had streaks of gray in it. The black iron handles and knobs—which Ellen had recommended—added a finishing touch, as did the cream wainscotting that went up to photo rail height, like the wainscotting in the dining room.

Ellen's favorite room—aside from the sunroom—was the room she called the library. Jason and his team hadn't done anything to it, but Ellen couldn't wait to help Sue decorate it and fill it with books.

Before he left, Jason carried the round, glass table and chairs up from the basement to the breakfast nook, so Ellen, Sue, and Tanya could have a place to sit and hang their coats while conducting another paranormal investigation. Ellen worried the natural light pouring in through the windows would contaminate anything recorded by her full-spectrum cameras, but she set them up anyway while Tanya lit candles and Sue took initial readings.

"Are we ready?" Ellen asked once the cameras were in position.

Tanya opened a box of crackers. "For the spirits. They smell like rosemary."

Ellen hadn't realized how hungry she felt. "Those sound delicious."

"You can have some, if you want," Tanya said with a smile. "Just be sure to leave some for the ghosts."

Ellen popped a cracker into her mouth. "Yum."

Sue held up the blindfold and headphones. "Who's going under this time?"

Tanya tilted her head. "Isn't it Ellen's turn?"

"I'd prefer to ask questions, but if you want me to, I will," Ellen conceded.

"No, that's okay. I'll do it." Tanya took the headphones and blindfold from Sue.

"You sure?" Ellen asked.

Tanya gave her a thumbs up before putting on the blindfold. Then she turned on the ghost box app and put on the noise-cancelling headphones.

"Can you hear me, Tanya?" Sue tested. When Tanya didn't reply, Sue announced, "Spirits of the other realm, we come in peace. We mean you no harm. We only wish to help you to find peace. If anyone is here with us today, please find the light of our candles and the smell of our snacks to guide you to our realm, so you can communicate with us. If you find your way here, please give us a sign."

"You can knock, make a light flicker, or touch that REM-POD on the kitchen floor to make it beep," Ellen instructed. "You can also use the shuffling radio broadcasts on that ghost box app to select the words you want to say to us."

Suddenly, Ellen heard that sound again—like mice were running through the walls.

"If there were mice here, Jason would have found them by now," Sue argued. "That's a sign from the spirit world."

"If that's you," Ellen began, "can you knock twice? If not, knock once."

Very distinctly, they heard two knocks.

Ellen and Sue glanced at each other with wide eyes.

"Is this Lucy?" Sue asked.

One knock.

"No?" Ellen whispered.

"Are you one of the people whose remains we discovered in the nearby cellar?" Sue questioned. "Please knock once for no and twice for yes."

One knock.

Ellen furrowed her brows. Who were they speaking with?

"What's your name?" Ellen asked. "Can you talk to us through our friend? Can you use the radio broadcasts to choose your words?"

Tanya's head slumped forward.

Ellen jumped to her feet and grabbed Tanya's shoulders. "Tanya? Are you okay?"

Ellen removed the blindfold to find Tanya's eyes closed. Ellen quickly removed the headphones. "Tanya?"

Tanya lifted her chin, and her eyes snapped open, but only the whites of her eyes were visible as she said, "My name is Hamilton."

Then, Tanya's head slumped forward again.

Sue stood up. "Tanya!"

Tanya blinked and looked up at them. "What happened?"

"Do you feel okay?" Sue asked.

"I'm fine," Tanya insisted. "Just tired. Did I fall asleep?"

Ellen gaped across the table at Sue. "Did we just speak with the ghost of Alexander Hamilton?"

Tanya was decidedly freaked out when she saw herself on the camera footage claiming to be Hamilton.

"I can't remember saying that. Do you think he possessed me?"

"He used you as a medium," Sue explained. "If he had possessed you, there'd be symptoms."

"I feel fine," Tanya insisted.

"Let's listen to the EVP recorder," Ellen suggested before rewinding and playing back the electronic voice phenomena recorder.

Nothing sounded unusual until Tanya said she was Hamilton.

"Play that back," Sue instructed Ellen.

Ellen rewound the recording, slowed it down, and turned up the volume. In the background of Tanya saying, "My name is Hamilton," were several whispers. One sounded like, "Get out." Another was clearly the word, "Evil." Other whispers were unintelligible.

"What was that about?" Tanya wondered.

"I don't know," Sue began, as she pulled out her laptop and opened it at the table. "But we've got to get to the bottom of it."

"Thirty-eight souls are trapped here," Tanya said. "We have to find a way to help them to find peace."

"I agree." Ellen opened her laptop, too. Almost everything she knew about Alexander Hamilton came from the popular Broadway musical. She decided to look him up to learn more about him.

"It says here that Hamilton didn't die until 1804," Ellen pointed out.

"We've been talking to more than one person," Sue reminded her. "Some died in 1778. Hamilton could still be haunting this place, even if he died later."

"Maybe he led a battle in this area and his men were killed," Tanya theorized. "And then he came back, hoping to help them find their way to the other side."

Ellen shook her head. "Bob said they were men, women, and children."

She and her friends spent the next several minutes in silence as they conducted research on their laptops.

"I'm finding a lot of hits about Hamilton in Williamsburg, but they deal mostly with finding ways to connect the musical with a tour of Colonial Williamsburg," Sue said after a while.

Tanya nodded. "It's like they're riding on the coattails of the musical's success. But why wouldn't they if it gets more people interested in history?"

"This site reminds readers about the relationships between Hamilton and the Marquis de Lafayette, George Washington, James Madison, and Thomas Jefferson—all who spent time in Williamsburg—but there's no mention of Hamilton himself leading any battles in the area. And there's nothing to connect him with the thirty-eight people haunting this house."

"I'm starving," Ellen admitted. "We need to check in and eat before our ghost tour tonight. Should we head out?"

"I'm hungry too," Tanya agreed. "Where should we eat?"

"I was hoping we'd return to the Fat Canary for lobster," Sue admitted.

"Oh, yes," Tanya exclaimed. "I've been craving that place since we last ate there. Ellen?"

"I'm not a fan of lobster, but I wouldn't mind getting the beef tenderloin Brian had last time. But I thought you had to have reservations."

Sue climbed to her feet. "Let's call on our way to check in. I'm looking forward to staying at the Brick House Shop. From the online photos, it looks quaint, and it's so conveniently located in the middle of Colonial Williamsburg."

"I'm looking forward to seeing it, too," Tanya agreed. "I wonder why your mother never stayed in one of the colonial houses. They all look so pretty online."

"First of all, I don't think they've been renting them out for that long," Sue explained. "But also, she liked getting away from the other tourists to a place more private."

"And, of course, don't forget the handsome Mr. Benson," Ellen chimed in.

Tanya laughed.

Sue shook her head. "I hope my mom isn't rolling around in her grave with all these jokes about her secret life."

"Knowing her, she's probably glad you finally know," Ellen theorized, "if, in fact, she and Mr. Benson ever had an affair."

As Ellen crossed the room for her purse, she heard running water.

"It turned on by itself," Tanya whispered, pointing to the kitchen sink with a trembling finger. "Just like before."

Ellen gawked as she watched steam rising from the hot water. Then, right before their eyes, letters were written on the window in the condensation: B-E-W-A-R-E.

"Beware of what?" Sue questioned.

Then another word followed: E-V-I-L.

Was Alexander Hamilton trying to warn them of something evil in the house?

CHAPTER SEVEN

The Ghost Tour and the Creeper

Ellen, Sue, and Tanya were disappointed not to secure a reservation at the Fat Canary, but while checking in at the Williamsburg Inn, their bellhop recommended the King's Arms Tavern, a bar and restaurant within walking distance of the Brick House Shop. Dressed in colonial attire—a long gray dress coat over a tan waistcoat with a white, frilly necktie, tight black breeches, white socks, and black dress shoes—the bellhop led them on his colonial bike. He sat on top of a large front wheel at least three feet in diameter, which he propelled with his pedals, along with a small back wheel, about a foot wide. Ellen and her friends followed in their car from the inn to their colonial house, where the hop helped them unload their bags and get settled in. As he did, he warned them that a ghost tour usually stopped at Wetherburn's Tavern—a historical building not currently in use just behind the house—but the tourists wouldn't stay long and knew to be quiet and courteous of the other guests.

"We're going to be on that very tour," Sue told him with a laugh.

The bellhop, a handsome man who appeared to be in his late twenties, combed his fingers through his long, brown hair, cut in colonial fashion. "Then you won't have far to go. Kimball Theatre, the meeting place, is just a ten-minute walk that way on Duke of Gloucester

Street," he pointed west, "and Duke of Gloucester is one block north of here, where the King's Arms Tavern is located."

Ellen clapped her hands. "Perfect!"

"I am glad to hear it," the bellhop said.

"So, why is this place called the Brick House Shop?" Tanya questioned the hop. "Were bricks once sold here?"

"No, madam," the hop replied. "It was originally built of brick. You saw the brick chimney? That is original. Later it burned and the chimney was the only part of the original structure that survived. During the renewal of the area in the thirties and forties, the building was reconstructed based on clues left behind by the colonists."

"Do you know what the building was used for?" Sue asked. "Was it a shop of some kind?"

"It was indeed a shop, madam. Two entrepreneurs by the names of Cosby and Moore used this place for what they called their Riding Car Business. They made wagons, wheels, and bicycles, like this one."

"How interesting." Ellen handed him a tip as he returned Moseby to her arms.

"Thank you, Madam. I hope you ladies enjoy your stay." The bellhop gave them a colonial bow and climbed onto his colonial bike and waved as he rode away.

"What a fun experience," Sue said once the bellhop had left. "Talk about immersive. And wasn't he cute? My heart kind of fluttered when he smiled at me."

Ellen and Tanya giggled.

"Oh, Sue," Ellen chastised. "He's not much older than Luke."

"So?"

"I thought there was something off about him," Tanya said.

Ellen opened her mouth with surprise. "Just because someone's different doesn't mean they're off."

Tanya shrugged. "He's definitely different."

"His physical beauty more than makes up for it," Sue argued.

"Well, this house is amazing," Tanya said, changing the subject. "Don't you think the outside resembles the house on Kestrel Court?"

"It really does," Sue agreed. "Cream exterior with black shutters—even the dormers look like mine."

"I like the black front door," Ellen noted. "I wonder if you might get Jason to paint yours black, too."

Sue tapped her chin with her index finger. "That's a good idea. Remind me to call him."

"Did you notice that the exterior light fixture was black iron?" Ellen asked smugly.

"I did," Sue replied with a grin. "Good call, Ellen. My house looks as colonial as is possible for a house built in 1983."

"We did good on the inside, too," Tanya pointed out. "This house has similar oak floors and white painted walls, and even the fireplace façade resembles yours."

"Now that we've properly patted ourselves on the backs," Sue began, "can we go eat? I'm starving."

As Ellen picked up her purse and coat from where she'd laid them on the blue leather sofa in the sitting room, she asked Tanya, "Do you want me to sleep down here on the pull-out or in the second double bed upstairs with you?"

Tanya shrugged. "Whatever you prefer."

"I like how y'all automatically assume I'm taking the bedroom with the big queen canopy bed downstairs," Sue teased.

Tanya put on her coat. "We know how much you hate stairs."

Ellen stepped through the front door, adding, "Plus, you snore worse than Tanya."

"I know that's true!" Sue laughed.

As they walked across the grassy lot in the chilly evening toward King's Arms Tavern, Tanya said, "I think our creeper is still following us. Do you guys sense him, too?"

Ellen nodded. "I think I've grown used to his presence. I don't think he's left us alone once."

"I don't think he has," Sue agreed.

"Do you think we're being followed by Alexander Hamilton?" Tanya wondered. "That would be pretty cool."

Ellen opened the door to the tavern for her friends. "I'm not sure, but I won't give up until we know."

Before she followed her friends inside, Ellen heard her phone ringing, so she dug it out of her purse and quickly answered it there on the front porch of the tavern. It was Bob Brooks calling, and she didn't want to miss any possible news from him. "Hello?"

"Hi, Ellen. Do you have a minute?"

"Of course. What's up?"

"My team and I have been studying the photos we took of the bones, and we've noticed something that the remains all have in common, something we missed while we were assembling the bodies."

"Really? What?"

"Marks across the fronts and backs of their skulls—the kind of marks caused by a sharp blade."

"What are you saying, Bob? What does that mean?"

"It means they were probably scalped."

Ellen covered her mouth and gasped. She stood there for a moment, processing what she'd just been told.

"Ellen, you there?"

"Yes. I'm here. How ghastly. You think every single one of them—the women and children too—were scalped?"

"Yes, I do. They were scalped and then left in that cellar to rot."

"Oh, how horrible. That's so terrible! I can't even imagine."

"People have done terrible things to one another—and still do."

"Well, thanks for letting me know. This will help with our investigation."

"I figured it would. I'll call again if we discover anything more. The DNA results should be in soon."

"Thanks, Bob. Goodbye."

When Ellen found her friends in one of the rooms of the tavern, they were sitting at a wooden table beside a cozy fireplace.

"What's happened?" Sue asked with a frown. "You're as white as a sheet."

Ellen removed her coat and sat down before telling them what Bob had reported to her over the phone.

Her friends covered their mouths, just as she had when she'd heard the news.

"I don't understand how Alexander Hamilton fits in with this story," Tanya said. "What did he have to do with a bunch of American colonists who were scalped?"

Ellen picked up her menu. "Let's question the creeper tonight."

After enjoying their peanut soup and "Mrs. Vobe's Tavern Dinner"—an herb- and garlic-crusted prime rib followed by "Jefferson's Bread Pudding"—Ellen and her friends walked up Duke of Gloucester Street to the Kimball Theatre to meet their ghost tour. They were surprised to discover that their guide was their very own bellhop, still wearing his colonial attire but now carrying a lantern.

"Hello, my good ladies," he said by way of greeting. "The look on your faces is priceless."

"Why didn't you say?" Ellen questioned him.

"Because I enjoy seeing that look of surprise," he replied with a smile. Then he added, "Allow me to introduce myself. I am Mr. Murphy—bellhop, actor, historian, and ghost enthusiast—at your service." He gave a little bow. "Hello again, Moseby."

Sue beamed at Ellen and Tanya, apparently happy to be in the company of Mr. Murphy again.

When a young couple arrived to join the tour, Mr. Murphy gave them the same speech about enjoying the look of surprise on their faces. He had been their bellhop, too.

With a total of ten people in the group—including Mr. Murphy—the tour began promptly at 8 p.m. In addition to Ellen and her friends and the younger couple who'd shared their bellhop, there was another couple who appeared to be in their forties, and two young women who were probably in their late twenties like their guide.

"Before we get started," Mr. Murphy began, "I have a serious question for you. I want you to think long and hard before you answer. Here goes: Why did the chicken go to the séance?"

"To get to the other side!" a young woman in the back of the group called out.

"Very good," Mr. Murphy said. "You passed the test. Now, we can begin."

Ellen and Tanya glanced at each other and shook their heads. This was a corny start to the tour. Hopefully, it wouldn't go downhill from there.

Mr. Murphy started with the history of the Kimball Theatre, which was originally built under a different name in the 1930's. Long before that, it was a private colonial home, and during the Civil War, was owned by the Wares.

"After the Battle of Williamsburg in 1862, there were wounded and dead everywhere the eye could see," Mr. Murphy narrated. "Mrs. Ware took in a wounded confederate soldier and attempted to help him, but he died that very day. She covered his body with a blanket and waited for the union forces to arrive. When they did, they commandeered her home into a hospital, which she welcomed. She told them it had already seen its first victim—a confederate soldier. She led the commanding officer to where the body lay, and when he lifted the blanket, the features on his face turned grim."

"'My brother,' the officer gasped, before throwing himself on the body and weeping."

"The brothers had joined opposite sides of the war. The surviving brother was killed in battle not long after; and, to this day, two civil war soldiers, one in blue and the other in gray, can be seen wandering this area, one brother in search of the other. People have witnessed them walk through walls and vanish in the street."

"How sad," Tanya whispered to Ellen.

From Kimball Theatre, their tour guide led them on a two-minute walk to the College of William and Mary, where they stood before a three-story, square brick structure called Brafferton Building. Mr. Murphy said that while it was used today as an administration building housing the office of the university president and provost, it was once an Indian school, where young Native Americans were forced from their homes and made to study English under harsh conditions and even harsher punishments if they rebelled.

"There was one boy that is rumored to have used a rope to climb from his third-floor window each night. He would run barefoot and bare-chested all over the grounds of the campus for hours until, exhausted, he would climb the rope back to his room and fall into bed. One night he was found dead on the grounds where he was known by some to run. While no one knows how he died, many speculated that he died of a broken heart. For nearly three hundred years, students, faculty, and administrators have seen an Indian boy running through the campus grounds at night, seeking the feeling of freedom he longed for when alive."

"This tour is making me sad," Tanya whispered to Ellen.

"Most ghost stories are sad," Ellen pointed out.

"Well, I was hoping to have fun, not be made to cry all night."

"Stop your whining and come on," Sue scolded with mock reproach.

Mr. Murphy led them a few minutes away to another part of the campus to a building called the President's House, which appeared to be a near replica of the Brafferton Building. Mr. Murphy's story soon revealed that they were built by the same architect, Henry Cary, who also built the Governor's Palace and other structures in Colonial Williamsburg.

"This is one of the few buildings in the area that has served the same purpose for which it was originally built nearly three hundred years ago," Mr. Murphy said. "It has served as the home to the university presidents and their families. For a brief time in 1781 during the final weeks of the American Revolution, it was commandeered by General Cornwallis and his British forces, who evicted the then university president, James Madison—cousin to the future president of the same name—and his family. A few weeks later, the house was used as a hospital for French officers wounded in the Battle of Yorktown, during which time a fire broke out. This may explain the presence of a French soldier who continued to roam the halls of this building for many decades. A third-floor closet door, in a room where one French officer was known to have died just before the fire, continually popped open of its own accord, no matter how often it was shut and locked. Over the decades, the same phenomenon was observed by one president's family after another. Then, one day in the 1960's, a work crew made a startling discovery. While working in the crawl space above the ceiling on the third floor, directly over the room with the famous closet door, workers found a human skeleton pressed into the brick wall. It was believed to be the remains of the French soldier who had died just before the fire broke out. It's speculated that the fire pressed him into the wall, and he was only found two hundred years later. From that point on, the closet door never mysteriously popped open again."

"Finally, a somewhat happy story," Tanya whispered. "The French officer found peace."

The tour left the William and Mary campus and headed back in the chilly night toward Duke of Gloucester Street, past the Kimball Theatre, to what was known as the George Wythe House. Ellen could sense the

Virginia creeper following them. She wondered if he enjoyed hearing stories about his colonial past—if he were indeed a colonial American, such as Alexander Hamilton.

Whereas the campus had been lit with electric streetlamps, Duke of Gloucester Street was lit with burning cressets. The larger buildings—like the Governor's Palace and George Wythe House—had candlelit lanterns on the steps, illuminating their façade.

As he stood with his lantern on the porch of the stately Wythe house, Mr. Murphy told his guests about a ghostly phenomenon that was consistently reported over the last nearly three hundred years—the sound of a peg leg going up the stairs, almost always at midnight.

"The sound is rumored to be made—not by a peg leg—but by the footfall of a high-heeled shoe followed by another stockinged foot belonging to a woman named Lady Ann Skipwith whose husband, she believed, preferred her sister, Jean. During a ball held at the Governor's Palace, Lady Skipwith, known for her fiery temper and proclivity toward speaking her mind, cursed out her husband for flirting with Jean and ran back to Wythe house, where she was staying as a guest. On the way, she lost one of her high-heeled shoes, but that didn't stop her from climbing the stairs at precisely midnight and flinging herself over the balcony to her death. Not long after, her husband married her sister, Jean."

"More tragedy," Tanya groaned.

Mr. Murphy overheard Tanya's comment and replied, "My dear lady, what I am about to tell you at Peyton Randolph House, just one block from here, is more tragic than anything I have told thus far. If you do not feel you can handle anymore tragedy, this might be a good time to call it a night."

Tanya's face turned as red as her sweater, and Ellen could tell that she did not appreciate being called out by Mr. Murphy, no matter how handsome he might be. With pursed lips, Tanya followed the group as they made their way to Peyton Randolph House.

"My feet are killing me," Sue complained to Ellen and Tanya. "How much further do you think we'll walk tonight?"

"Quit your whining and come on," Tanya teased, as payback for Sue's earlier comment.

"Touché," Sue replied with a grin.

Ahead of them in the cool night, Mr. Murphy said, "This next house has been visited by many famous people—George Washington, Thomas Jefferson, the Marquis de Lafayette, Alexander Hamilton, Comte de Rochambeau, and many more."

"Did you say Alexander Hamilton?" Sue asked.

"Indeed, madam. Follow me."

CHAPTER EIGHT

The Ghosts of Peyton Randolph House

Except for the Governor's Palace, Peyton Randolph House was the largest building Ellen had seen in Colonial Williamsburg. Painted a deep red—including the door and shutters—this two-story L-shaped building was as stately as it was ominous.

Ellen was surprised when Mr. Murphy opened the door and invited the group inside, since up until then they had remained outside of each building. Waiting for them was a black woman wearing colonial attire; however, her clothing reflected that worn by a slave.

"Welcome," she greeted. "Come on inside. My name is Jacinda Bloom. Welcome to Peyton Randolph House, home of the most prominent family in Virginia. Mr. Peyton Randolph was highly regarded and an important contributor to the founding of our nation. He was the first president of the continental congress. Had he lived long enough, he might have been our first elected president. He died in 1775."

Ellen immediately sensed oppression stifling her in the beautiful entryway. It was the same feeling she had gotten when she and her friends had visited with their spouses.

"In this house, there are two worlds living under one roof—the powerful gentry and leaders of a revolution for freedom, and the twenty-seven men, women, and children who are enslaved and who live solely to serve their masters. Ironic, don't you think?"

This was a different presentation than their previous guide had given them when Ellen and her friends had come with their spouses in the light of day, and at night it felt like a different house.

Jacinda led the group from one room to another and gave details about how each room was used—such as the closet where Mrs. Peyton gave her slave, Eve, her orders for the day—orders that included the duties for the other enslaved, such as what meals to cook. In the previous tour, Ellen and her group had been told about the rooms, but this tour told it from the slaves' perspective.

Jacinda showed them the slave quarters, where their living began at night, when their masters slept—though many of them slept on pallets outside of their masters' doors, ready to serve when called. She showed them the parlor, study, office, bedrooms, and a big kitchen, which she said was second in size only to the Governor's Palace.

"Every room meant for the gentry is built to express the great wealth accumulated by the Randolph family, which was only possible because of the labor they owned. In contrast to these beautiful rooms with their inlaid, painted wood panels, coal-burning fireplace, and finest draperies are the plain, even stark, rooms for the enslaved."

Jacinda pointed to portraits of Peyton and Elizabeth Randolph—almost as large as paintings found in the Governor's Palace—and emphasized that their purpose was to communicate wealth and status.

"This was important because they hosted many political leaders during the revolution: Patrick Henry, Thomas Jefferson, George Washington, James Madison, Alexander Hamilton, the Marquis de Lafayette, Comte de Rochambeau, and many others talking about the need to get out from under the thumb of tyranny and oppression while twenty-seven enslaved people under this roof listened."

She led them to another bed chamber. "Next to the one where the Randolphs' sons resided while on holiday from William and Mary is the chamber for Elizabeth Harrison, Mrs. Randolph's niece. She comes here at age thirteen after her parents are killed, and she becomes orphaned. Mrs. Randolph is going to teach this young girl how to run a household, how to control her people, the enslaved. Mrs. Randolph will pass all that she knows onto her niece, so she can thrive within the institution of slavery."

Jacinda pulled out a rolled-up pallet in the sitting room outside of Elizabeth Harrison's room. "This is where Violet will sleep, outside of Elizabeth Harrison's door, ready to attend to her needs. Violet is the same age as Elizabeth. Both girls are at the same point in their childhood, but one will learn how to control the other, and the other will learn how to be controlled."

Ellen shuddered—not only from the dark past of America being brought to light by the eloquent Jacinda, but also from a cold and creepy presence that she felt enter the room.

"Thank you, Jacinda," Mr. Murphy said. "And now I would like to inform our guests of the paranormal history of the house, which is considered by many to have been cursed, possibly by Elizabeth Randolph's slave, Eve, after being punished for attempting to run away with the British. Her punishment was to be sold to different owners, separating her from her son. Whether she is the cause, no one knows for certain, but few dispute the fact that the house is cursed. Wouldn't you agree, Jacinda?"

"I would agree the house is cursed," Jacinda conceded, "however your version of the story of Eve is the white one. People in the black community believe a different version. They say that Eve was captured by British forces and after a prisoner exchange, she was sold to another owner, having already been replaced in the Randolph household. In this version, Eve returns in spirit to watch over her son and becomes trapped by the curse."

Mr. Murphy nodded. "Even the Marquis de Lafayette experienced paranormal phenomena in this house. After a visit here, he is known to have said, 'Upon my arrival, as I entered through the foyer, I felt a hand on my shoulder. It nudged me as if intending to keep me from entering. I quickly turned but found no one there. The nights were not restful as the sounds of voices kept me awake for most of my stay.'"

"And tragedies abound in this house," Mr. Murphy continued. "Since it was built in 1715, at least thirty people are known to have died from suicide, freak accidents, and other inexplicable causes. One gentleman shot himself in front of the fireplace in the drawing room. A boy fell to his death from a tree in the front yard. A girl fell out of an upstairs window. A confederate veteran attending the College of William and Mary suddenly fell and died on this very spot. Two men staying at the house got into a fight and shot and killed each other. A servant was pushed to her death from the top of the stairs."

"Lots of people have been pushed down the stairs," Jacinda interjected. "Even modern-day employees."

"Yes. And at least three children committed suicide. And the list goes on."

Sue whispered to Ellen, "I wonder if a Shinigami is at work."

"Could be," she replied.

"When this place was used as a guest house," Jacinda continued, "many reported having been awakened by a woman wearing a white cap at the foot of their bed in the oak-paneled room, urging them to leave. Some guests took her advice and fled from the house in their pajamas."

"People have heard bootsteps, crashing glass, knocks, moans, the sounds of children playing, a woman singing outside, and other unexplainable noises," Mr. Murphy continued, "but the woman is the most reported phenomenon. She's seen in the oak-paneled room, always at the foot of the bed, urging the guests to leave."

"Many believe that woman to be Eve." Jacinda waved her arm, beckoning the guests to follow. "Now we will attempt to speak with her in the oak-paneled room. Come with me."

The group followed Jacinda and Mr. Murphy down a hall to the back of the house into a room with a four-poster queen bed and two wingback chairs flanking a fireplace.

The room felt significantly colder than the rest of the house. Even with her coat on, Ellen had chills.

"We believe this was the master," Jacinda began, "but we don't know for sure. As you can see, it has blue-painted inlaid oak panels on the walls, just like we saw in the parlor downstairs, along with a coal-burning fireplace, and beautiful silk rug. At the foot of this bed, this is where the white-capped woman appears."

"Sometimes she will make her presence known to a tour group by knocking on the wall or moving the bedding. Let us see if she will honor us with her presence tonight." Mr. Murphy raised his arms. "We call upon the white-capped woman. Please give us a sign that you're here with us."

Several people in the group took out their phones to record the summoning. Sue decided to do the same.

"Shoot, my phone's dead," Sue complained.

"Mine, too," a woman behind them said.

Ellen and Tanya checked their phones. Their batteries were drained.

"Something touched me," a young woman in the back whispered.

"It wasn't me," her friend insisted.

The woman in her forties standing close behind Ellen gasped and whispered, "Wh-what's that?"

Ellen turned to see the woman pointing to the corner of the room where a faint white cap appeared and then vanished. One of the guests—the younger married woman—fled the room.

"Is that you, Eve?" Mr. Murphy asked. "If so, please knock once for yes or twice for no."

One knock.

Another guest left the room, while another accused, "This is a prank, right?"

Just then, the face—only the face—of a black woman with a white cap floated from the corner and stopped before Ellen.

Beside Ellen, Tanya shrieked.

The disembodied face moved her mouth and whispered, "He is evil. Get away from him."

Then she disappeared.

It took Ellen a full twenty seconds to gather her wits. She was shaking from head to toe, the hair on the back of her neck standing on end.

After a beat, Jacinda exclaimed, "Oh, my heavens! I've never seen her speak!"

"I don't believe it," the man in his forties murmured. "That had to be a trick."

"I hope someone caught that on camera," Mr. Murphy gasped as he glanced around the room wearing a look of excitement.

"I got it," the young man behind Sue said. "Check it out."

"Oh, wow." Ellen covered her mouth in disbelief as she watched the face of a black woman wearing a white cap appear on the man's phone screen.

The man with the phone showed the video again to others in their group. "That was so messed up. I've got goosebumps! I wish my wife would have stayed to see it. Honey?"

The young man went looking for his wife.

"What do you think she meant?" a girl in the back asked.

Ellen had the feeling that the woman in the white cap was warning her about the creeper that had been following her and her friends around Williamsburg.

"She likes to warn guests of the evil in this house," Jacinda explained. "Perhaps we should take her advice and go."

From the Peyton Randolph House, the group—garrulous now that they'd seen and heard a ghost (most of them for the first time)—walked with renewed vigor down Nicholson Street toward the Public Jail, which Mr. Murphy estimated was ten minutes away.

As they walked, Ellen caught up to Jacinda and said, "I'm surprised not to see a lot of paranormal investigators out tonight. Do you get many of them here?"

"Oh, no. It's not allowed. The board of trustees doesn't want a bunch of ghost hunters stirring up the guests—either the living or the dead. Only sanctioned tour guides are allowed to commune with the spirits of Colonial Williamsburg."

"I see." Ellen was glad she hadn't already mentioned that she and her friends were paranormal investigators. Rather than say so now, she asked, "This is going to sound like a strange question, but do you know of any reason why someone might consider Alexander Hamilton evil? Are there any stories that you know painting him in a negative light?"

"Not Alexander Hamilton, no," Jacinda replied. "But Henry Hamilton, that's a different story. We talk about him briefly at the Public Jail."

Ellen felt the hair on the back of her neck stand on end again. She looked behind her, and although she saw Sue and a few others from the group casually strolling after her, she sensed the creeper and his agitation.

Ellen turned back to Jacinda. "Who was Henry Hamilton?"

"A lieutenant-governor in the British army. You'll hear more about him tonight."

Tanya, walking beside Ellen, asked, "Could Eve have been warning us about him?"

"It's very possible," Jacinda admitted. "According to legend—you won't find this in the history books—Eve is the one who gave him the name that history most remembers him by."

Sue, trying to keep up behind them, asked, "What name is that?"

"The Hair Buyer," Jacinda said. "He was called that because he rewarded native peoples for bringing him the scalps of American rebels."

Ellen broke out in a cold sweat. "Did you say *scalps?*"

"That's right," Jacinda confirmed.

Sue grabbed Ellen and Tanya by their arms. "That night over the sink, when the men were here, remember? After I closed on the house. It wasn't *The* Home *Buyer Beware* that was written over the kitchen sink."

"It was *The* Hair *Buyer*," Tanya finished.

Jacinda, who hadn't heard their whispered exchange, continued, "Henry Hamilton was detained in the very jail we're walking toward."

"Would you mind telling us everything you know about him?" Ellen asked the eloquent tour guide. "We'd be happy to pay you for your time."

"Unfortunately, my knowledge on the subject is limited," Jacinda confessed. "All I know is that legend has it that when Eve was rescued during the prisoner exchange, she and her fellow prisoners reported witnessing their jailer, Lieutenant-Governor Henry Hamilton, accepting human scalps, which he callously called 'dried meat,' from Delaware Indians who'd been recruited to support the British cause. I also know that when Hamilton and his fellow officers were captured and brought to Virginia to await their fate, Governor Thomas Jefferson decided not to treat them as gentlemen prisoners of war, as was customary at the time. Rather, they were locked in iron chains and imprisoned like common criminals."

Ellen felt a hand on her shoulder, and, assuming it was Sue, she turned to find no one there.

Sue, who had fallen in line behind Tanya, noticed. "Everything okay?"

Shrugging, Ellen folded her arms across her chest and picked up her pace.

The Public Gaol (pronounced "jail") was an old-looking red brick structure with an open brick-paved courtyard surrounded by four cells, each about ten feet by ten feet in size. Jacinda explained that thieves, runaway slaves, debtors, and traitors were held there, sometimes for years, before they were fined, branded, or hanged.

One of the wooden-clad cells had a view of the gallows. All of them had chains bolted to the walls and "thrones," or privies with steps to a high bench with a hole in it.

Mr. Murphy told the story of the fifteen infamous pirates who were Blackbeard's henchmen, captured and held prisoner there in 1718. "In the following decades, inmates used to complain of the eerie sounds at night of pirates goading one another."

He went on to talk about the famous Hair Buyer, Lieutenant-Governor Henry Hamilton of the British armed services, who was captured in 1779 and imprisoned here in chains with six of his fellow men for eighteen months—something that was rarely done with officers.

"Governor Thomas Jefferson believed such treatment was necessary for punishing the British lieutenant-governor for his savage treatment of American colonists," Jacinda explained. "Hamilton was known as the Hair Buyer because he purchased white scalps from Native Americans sympathetic to the crown."

Mr. Murphy added, "Some paranormal enthusiasts have claimed to have been in communication with his spirit here in Williamsburg. They say he asks for help, but none have figured out why."

As Ellen followed the group from the final cell, she felt cold breath against her ear, followed by, "Help." Jumping away, she bumped into Sue.

"Sorry," Ellen said to her friend, who'd come close to falling.

"Did something happen?" Sue asked.

"I'll tell you later," Ellen promised, anxious to get back to their rental house.

From the Public Gaol, the group was led past the Capitol Building to Duke of Gloucester Street along a string of taverns—only one of which was still in use, the King's Arms Tavern, where they had dined earlier that evening. Ellen couldn't hear what her tour guides were saying as they stood outside of Wetherburn's Tavern, because she was too shaken over all that had happened to her that night, and she wanted only to return to her room where she could sit inside a circle of protection and research the Hair Buyer on her laptop. She needed to better understand Henry Hamilton and why he was following her. Did he want to possess her? Or was he trying to tell her something?

CHAPTER NINE

Hamilton

Outside the Brick House Shop, after they'd left their ghost tour, Ellen said to her friends, "Before we go inside, we need to let the creeper know he isn't permitted to follow us."

"You think it's the Hair Buyer?" Tanya asked. "It could be someone trying to warn us about Hamilton."

"I don't want to take any chances," Ellen replied. "When we were leaving the jail, I heard 'Help.' I swear. It was clear as day."

"Why didn't you say?" Tanya wanted to know.

"I was too frazzled. Anyway, I think the creeper wants our help, whoever he is. That must be why he keeps following us."

"It was fun having him around when we thought he was Alexander," Sue admitted. "But now I'm freaked out, especially when I think of how he followed my mom."

Ellen took a deep breath and proclaimed to the air, "You can't follow us inside. Whoever's been following us around Virginia—whether you're Henry Hamilton or someone else—you are not allowed to stay here with us. We banish you from our company."

After they had crossed the threshold, Ellen poured salt in the doorway before closing and locking the door.

Her friends were hanging their coats on the hooks in the entryway, so Ellen did the same. "Let's hope that worked."

"What's that on your back?" Tanya asked Ellen. "Did you scratch yourself?"

"Where?" Ellen turned to Tanya.

"Oh, gawd." Sue pulled down Ellen's sweater in the back. "I don't think she can reach there. Can you, Ellen?"

"Take a photo and show me," Ellen pleaded, feeling a wave of nausea sweep over her. "Oh, my gosh, show me!"

Tanya took the photo with her phone and handed it to Ellen. Just above her bra strap, where the neckline of her sweater scooped down, there were four red lines about a quarter-inch thick and four inches long. They looked like scratches made by a human hand.

"What in the world!" Ellen gasped. "I didn't feel anything. How could that have happened?"

"Maybe the creeper was trying to get your attention," Sue speculated.

"What could he possibly want with me?" Ellen wondered. "I mean, he's not after my scalp, is he?"

"We need some answers," Tanya said. "As tired as I am, I won't be able to sleep until we learn more about this guy."

"Why don't I make a pot of coffee?" Ellen offered, still shaken by the scratches. She was determined to figure out what she was dealing with.

"That sounds good," Sue said. "I also have that box of chocolates I bought today at the Wythe Candy Shop. I just might share it with y'all if you're nice to me."

"When are we anything but nice to you?" Tanya challenged.

"That attitude right there isn't very nice, now is it," Sue teased.

Tanya rolled her eyes as she grabbed her laptop and sat in the corner of the blue leather couch.

Once they had their coffee, chocolates, and circle of protection, they got to work.

Not long into the research, Sue said, "It says here that Henry was the lieutenant-governor of Canada and the British commander of Fort

Detroit during the American Revolution. He was captured in 1779 by George Rogers Clark during a raid into modern-day Indiana. Then he was brought here to Williamsburg where he was treated very poorly as a prisoner because of his practice of purchasing human scalps from Indian allies. It says that he was freed in a prisoner exchange in 1781, after which he returned to Canada as lieutenant-governor and deputy governor of Quebec. Later, he served as the governor of Bermuda and governor of Dominica until he died in 1796 on the island of Antigua." Sue looked up at her friends. "That doesn't really explain why his spirit would return to Williamsburg."

"No, it doesn't," Ellen agreed before popping a chocolate into her mouth.

"I found something interesting," Tanya piped up. "This article talks about Henry's relationship with the Native Americans. It says he began as an artistic observer. Apparently, he was somewhat of an artist who made dozens of sketches of indigenous people, along with landscapes. Anyway, this article says that although Henry referred to Indians as 'the savages,' he became skilled at communicating and trading with them and sometimes dressed in their clothing and wore their paint and participated in their dance ceremonies to show his political alignment with them."

"That's what I'm reading," Ellen said, before taking a sip of her coffee. "But this article goes on to say how he paid the Indians for the scalps. The Indians would first capture a group of American settlers, lead them with their belongings to the outskirts of a city, where the Indians would either tomahawk and scalp their victims or just scalp them before dumping their bodies and keeping their loot. Then they would present the scalps to Hamilton as proof."

"That's what happened to our thirty-eight victims." Tanya covered her face with her hands and shuddered. "Gosh, I can only imagine."

Ellen began to suspect that Tanya was an empath. She seemed to feel the emotional trauma of the ghosts.

Sue shook her head. "It's too horrible to imagine."

"I can understand why the victims would reach out to us," Ellen reasoned. "But what could Henry Hamilton possibly want with us? Why would he need help?"

"I don't know, but this is promising," Sue began. "This website claims that the journals of Henry Hamilton are held in the rare books collection at the library at the College of William and Mary."

"Really?" Ellen felt a surge of excitement course through her.

Tanya straightened her back. "We should go tomorrow to read them!"

"That's what I was thinking," Ellen agreed. "Maybe his writing will shed some light on why he's here in Williamsburg and what he wants from us."

Sue, who had bent over her laptop, said, "It looks like it's about a twenty-minute walk from here."

"That's not bad," Tanya pointed out. "Unless your feet are bothering you again."

"Let's see how they feel in the morning," Sue said. "But whether we walk or drive, we should plan to eat breakfast at the library. There's an Aromas inside, and they have a delicious menu."

"Sounds like a plan," Ellen said excitedly.

"Should we make our circles of protection and go to bed?" Tanya wondered. "I haven't sensed him lately, but just to be safe."

Ellen turned to Sue. "Are you sure you don't want to sleep upstairs with us?"

Sue shook her head. "Those stairs look treacherous. I'd rather take my chances with the creeper."

Although Ellen was tired, she felt nervous, keyed-up, and awake from the excitement of the evening and from the coffee she'd consumed while reading about Hamilton. Not wanting to keep Tanya awake, who slept in the other double bed a few feet away from her, she texted Brian, in case he was up.

"Moseby and I miss you," he wrote.

"I miss you, too," she texted back. "Be home soon."

They texted their love and good-night wishes, and then Ellen rolled over on her side to try to sleep. She wished she had brought Mo with her. The feel of his warm, cuddly body beside her would have been a comfort. If anyone were to ask, she wouldn't know whom she missed more—Brian or Mo.

After a surprisingly uneventful night of sleep, Ellen and her friends readied themselves for their visit to Swem Library—the library on the campus of William and Mary and home to Aromas specialty coffees and dining.

Tanya and Ellen had convinced Sue that a twenty-minute walk would be a nice way to start the day, but as soon as they stepped out of the Brick House Shop, Ellen immediately sensed the presence of the creeper.

Despite his presence, it was a beautiful day for a walk. The clear blue sky, gentle breeze, and forty-degree temperature invigorated Ellen. Other tourists were out enjoying the day, too. Mr. Murphy passed them on his colonial bike and gave them a wave.

About ten minutes later, Mr. Murphy caught up to them again on his bike just as they were approaching the Kimball Theatre.

"That was truly something last night, ladies," he said by way of greeting. "I have never seen anything like that before, and I have been conducting these tours for over three years."

"We have a knack for attracting the spirits," Sue confessed.

Ellen added, "Each time we visit Virginia, we're followed by the same creeper."

"At first we thought he was Alexander Hamilton," Tanya said.

"What made you think that?" Mr. Murphy, who now walked his bike alongside them, asked.

They waited for a family with small children to pass them on the sidewalk. Then Ellen replied, "He told us his name was Hamilton—or at least someone did. We aren't sure if the ghost talking to us was the same as the one following us."

"He told you? How?"

Tanya blushed. "He used me as a medium."

"You're a medium?"

"Not usually, no—though I was possessed once."

"Technically, it was an attachment," Sue reminded her.

"Well, I came very close to being possessed," Tanya stated with a smirk.

They came up to a crosswalk and waited for traffic to clear before crossing the street to the college campus.

Mr. Murphy crossed the street with them. "Are you touring the college today?"

"No," Sue replied. "We're going to read the journals of Henry Hamilton. We think he may be the creeper following us."

"Is he following you now?"

"Oh, yes," Tanya insisted. "Don't you feel him, guys?"

Ellen nodded.

"Unfortunately, yes," Sue affirmed.

"How would you ladies like to join me for a séance at Peyton Randolph House later tonight?"

Ellen and her friends exchanged looks of surprise.

"We didn't think paranormal investigators were allowed," Ellen pointed out.

"Unsanctioned ones aren't allowed," he clarified. "I am sanctioning you this very minute."

"Count us in." Sue beamed.

"What time?" Tanya wanted to know.

"It will have to be late, after my ghost tour. Would ten o'clock work?"

"We'll be there," Ellen assured him.

"Great. See you then." Mr. Murphy hopped on his bike and rode off, giving them a wave as he left.

"How exciting," Sue said as they continued across the campus toward the library. "I wonder if there's anything in particular that he's hoping to discover."

"I was wondering the same thing," Tanya admitted.

As they approached a sunken garden, Ellen remarked, "This campus is so beautiful. Look at the garden. And those buildings are so full of charm."

They followed a winding path beneath red and orange tree canopies and past old, stately brick buildings with pretty gardens planted near their entrances.

"Isn't this the oldest college in the United States?" Sue wondered.

"I think it is." Tanya took out her phone. After a moment, she added, "No, it's the second oldest. Harvard has it beat by about thirty years."

Soon they came upon another lovely garden. It was geometrical with a large sundial at its center and a wide, red-brick pathway leading up to the library. Three stories high and made of brick, the library entrance and the path leading up to it were flanked by tall, colorful trees, the leaves of which had turned to gorgeous reds, oranges, and yellows. The building itself appeared more modern than some of the other structures on campus. High above the main entrance was a circular window at least eight feet in diameter framed with rings and spokes.

The entryway was surprisingly modern. Ellen and her friends were disappointed to discover that Aromas was an outlet of the restaurant without full dining service. But they were able to get specialty coffee and breakfast sandwiches, which they enjoyed before making their way to the rare books collection on the other side of the first floor.

They were greeted by a woman who appeared to be in her late sixties. Her thin, white hair was worn in a short bob, and she was small and pear-shaped with bright blue eyes and an infectious smile. After Ellen explained what they were looking for, the woman, who introduced herself as Ann Devlin, became even more excited.

"Let me show you where they are." Ann jumped from behind the reception desk to lead them to the special stacks. "Is there anything specific that you want to know about Henry Hamilton? I happen to be a scholar of Virginia history, specializing in the era of the American Revolution, and I know quite a lot about him."

"We want to know everything about him," Ellen said. "Do you have time for an interview?"

"I have all the time in the world." Ann beamed. "Let me take you to a reading room where we can look at the journals and talk privately."

Ann pulled a pair of gloves from her blazer pockets and put them on before taking six books from the rare books shelf. Then, she led Ellen and her friends past the shelves to a door to a room made mostly of windows. They sat on one end of a long conference table.

"Are you ladies writing a book?" Ann asked as she opened the first journal.

"No—though I've always wanted to," Sue admitted. "Our interests are motivated by something more personal."

Ann tilted her head to the side. "Is one of you related to Henry Hamilton?"

Ellen chuckled and shook her head. "We think we're being followed by his ghost." Then she quickly added, "We know not everyone is a believer in the supernatural, so you won't offend us if you think we're delusional."

Sue scoffed. "Speak for yourself."

"You can't live in Williamsburg and be a skeptic," Ann stated. "They surround us here. One can't get away from them."

"Well, this one has been a bit more insistent," Tanya explained. "We're trying to figure out what he wants from us."

"I'm afraid I don't know the answer to that," Ann said with a frown. "But I can tell you what I know of Henry Hamilton. As the lieutenant-governor of Detroit, he was positioned to be the primary contact with the Native Americans in the west during the Revolutionary War. When he received orders from the crown to solicit the help of indigenous people against the rebels, he followed them. And having dealt with them early in his career when he fought in the Seven Years War, he understood the importance of their ceremonies and rituals, and he respected them—or at least pretended to—and in so doing earned their trust."

Ann opened the first journal and placed it in front of Sue, who sat at the end of the table with Ellen and Tanya on either side. The three friends looked over the first page. The first entry read, "August 6th. 1778. Mr. Francis Maisonville arrived at Detroit from the Illinois with an account of the attack of Kaskaskias by the Americans. The officer who commanded the party had made Monsieur de Rocheblave prisoner. The officer confined him in his own house and laid him in irons—no opposition made by the inhabitants."

Almost daily entries reported the occurrences of each day—a scout arrived with a message from a general with intel about the rebels, another Native tribe arrived and swore their allegiance, tents were struck, a march ensued, bad weather was endured, a tribe hosted a feast, speeches were given, and provisions arrived.

Ann turned the pages with her gloved fingers, saying, "Notice how he continually refers to the indigenous people as 'the Savages,' and yet listen to this entry, dated October 14, 1778, when he writes, 'By the way, no reproachful or angry expression falls from any native when another makes a mistake or fails any way in his duty; he is either calmly set to right by an old man, or perhaps the young men may titter, for the most trifling thing is matter of laugh to an Indian. Let it be remarked that there is no such thing in use among them, not even to be found in their language, as an oath or a curse—terms of reproach they have few—*hog* is most common.'"

Ann commented, "That doesn't sound very savage to me. Does it to you?"

Ellen shook her head. "I see what you mean. These Native Americans didn't overreact to mistakes and never cursed. The worst thing they called someone was hog. They sound pretty civil in this account."

Ann turned the page. "Further down in the same entry, he writes, 'Before a morsel was touched, the priest made a short address to the Master of life. At the close of each division of his harangue, all the Indians joined in one solemn expression of assent. The priest then in more particular terms addressed the Lord of all, imploring his protection in their present undertaking and besought the inferior spirits presiding over rivers, woods, and mountains, to be propitious. The deepest silence and most serious attention were observable during the prayer, no such thing as laughing or whispering, so common in our places of worship. It was a clear starlit night, and I was affected by the humble and reverential worship of these poor ignorant but well-meaning creatures.'"

Ann lifted her eyes from the page. "From his words, you can sense the admiration he feels for the natives, and yet he still thinks of them as 'poor ignorant but well-meaning creatures.'"

Ann turned another page. "And now see here, where he describes another interaction with the Indians. He writes, 'The Savages having saluted us last night on our arrival, we returned their compliment this morning with three rounds from the six-pounder. Fourteen of their warriors presenting themselves to join us, I thanked them for their goodwill, and taking off my war belt, joined it to that of their Chief, and sang the War Song.'"

Ann interjected, "Isn't it interesting that he knows how to sing their war song? Then he adds, 'They said they would follow me wherever I went, though I had broken an old custom, in not pouring some rum on the grindstone which was to sharpen the war axe. I owned myself in fault and ordered two bottles of rum. This with the delay of issuing provision delayed us 'till ten o'clock. The Grande Glaize is a river larger than the Severn at Gloucester and subject to sudden and violent floods. Night coming on, we were obliged to encamp a league and half below our destined station.'"

"He honored their custom," Tanya pointed out, "even though it delayed their travels."

Ann turned another page. "Then on the twenty-seventh, he writes, 'Some Pouteouattamies from St. Joseph arrived with Louison Chevalier and the Old Chief Nanaquìbé. The chiefs of the Lake Indians came in the evening to my tent and talked upon the belt of the Chickasaws sent to the Shawnees and Delawares, and by them to the Miamis, which they produced. The purport of this belt was to exhort them to unite for the purpose of repelling the Virginians and to invite the other nations to join them. They also produced the string which the Virginians had sent to the Indians on the Ouabache, informing them of their intention of going to Detroit, and seizing me and my company. It appears the Old Tobacco and his son (called the young Tobacco) are strong with the Virginians. The Grande Coéte (a Peankasháa chief) had declared he should act in conformity with his elder brothers, meaning the Quiquaboes and Ouiattanons. The Spaniards advised the Indians, including the Powhatans, not to credit the Virginians on their assurances, as they are incapable from their poverty to make good their promises. Egushewai told me the Miamis were desirous of having an axe presented to them. I agreed to it.'

"So, you can see he has dealings with many, many tribes and seems to understand their various customs and expectations," Ann pointed out. "In other papers, he says he has learned to speak many of the tribal languages—not fluently, but enough to be effective. He has a good relationship with them."

"Yes, it seems so," Sue agreed. "But is it true that he paid them for the scalps of men, women, and children?"

"I'm afraid it is," Ann conceded. "In his earlier letters, he writes how deplorable he finds the customs of Indian warfare, and he insists that unarmed men, women, and children be spared. He writes that the ways of the natives constituted a kind of brutality from which civilization had long since rescued the white race. And he notes that he cannot control it. He even petitions his superiors for more troops to deter the natives from indiscriminate killing."

"But he encouraged it," Ellen insisted. "He rewarded it."

"Yes," Ann said again. "When he was presented with scalps, he didn't ask about their origins. He accepted them with gratitude and usually made gifts of them to other tribes."

Ann showed them a few more entries that she found fascinating—mostly describing the customs of the Native Americans—and then opened the final journal, which recorded Hamilton's march from Vincennes to Williamsburg as a prisoner of war.

"He describes the ravages of both the elements and the Americans. Here, on June 30, 1779, he writes, 'I landed with Major Hay and Mr. Bellefeuille on the east side of the river to get a view of the destruction occasioned by a hurricane. We had some difficulty in scrambling to the top of the cliff. Great crags and large trees tumbled together in confusion, obliging us sometimes to creep and sometimes to climb.'

"And then here, on the thirtieth, he writes, 'We were put into a log house and received the compliments of the people on our arrival, expressed by discharging their pieces almost all day long. This joy of theirs at our capture made us recollect what C.C. had told us, that we should run the risk of our lives in passing the frontier.'

"Then on the fifth, he writes, 'Had a very fatiguing march. Our guides lost themselves and misled us.' And on the tenth, he says, 'We were delayed here much against our will thinking we held our lives by a very precarious tenure, for the people on our first coming looked upon us as little better than the Savages, which was very excusable considering how we had been represented, and besides that they had suffered very severely from the violence of those people.'

"And twenty miles or so later, he adds on the nineteenth, 'Captain Logan, the person commanding here, had had his arm broken by a buckshot in a skirmish with them and was not yet recovered. The people here were not exceedingly well disposed to us, and we were accosted by the females especially in pretty coarse terms. But the Captain and his wife, who had a brother carried off by the Indians, were very civil and hospitable.'"

The diary entries described the nearly insurmountable hills, slippery from rain, that the prisoners marched over, along with the ravaging winds and long, arduous river crossings. Some of their hosts were hospitable and others were adversarial. And, by the time they arrived in Williamsburg, Hamilton and his fellow prisoners were spent.

Ann pointed to an entry dated June 16. Ellen and her friends read, "About Sunset, we reached Williamsburg—wet, jaded, dispirited, and forming ideas of what sort of judicial examination we were to undergo. By the time we reached the Palace (as it is called), the Governor's residence, our escort of curious persons had become very numerous. The officer went in to give account of his mission, and we remained on horseback before the door expecting the civilities naturally to be looked for from a man the first in place of the province. In half an hour not finding our expectations answered, I flung myself from my horse, fatigued and mortified to be left a spectacle to a gazing crowd."

"We read in other sources," Sue began, "that Thomas Jefferson wasn't too happy with Hamilton."

"No," Ann confirmed.

Ellen sighed. "As interesting as all of this is, it still doesn't answer our questions. If he died in the Caribbean, why did his ghost return here? And why is he relentlessly pestering us—and Sue's mom before us—to help him?"

Ann scratched her head. "There is one passage that may shed some light on that." She turned the page to an entry marked August 7, 1779, where Hamilton writes, 'Even should I manage to survive the poor conditions of this miserable cell, I fear my ghost shall forever haunt it. The march through the frontier forced me to revisit settlements harassed by my Indian allies on my orders. Hearing their curses and their laments, their losses, and their grief chipped away at my soul until I am quite certain there is nothing left. Those poor, pitiful people have suffered far more than I and my men, even as we lie here on the ground in the stink of our own filth. I shall forever feel sorry for the part I played in adding to the toll of human suffering.'"

"Wow," Tanya said with a gasp. "He sounds sincerely sorry."

"But sorry isn't enough," Sue declared. "It's too little, too late. What does he expect us to do about it?"

Ellen shook her head. "I don't know, but I hope he doesn't expect forgiveness from his victims. He's already asked too much of them to demand that, too."

A loud clatter just outside the room made all four women jump in their seats. Ann hurried through the door to investigate.

When she returned, she had a thick book with her. "This fell of its shelf. I looked around, and there's no one else here."

"What is it?" Ellen asked.

Ann glanced at its cover. "It's an atlas of Virginia."

"Do you think Henry caused that book to fall?" Tanya asked her friends.

"If he did," Sue began, "why?"

CHAPTER TEN

Eve

That night, Ellen and her friends bundled up in their coats for the five-minute walk to the Peyton Randolph House carrying totes with their cameras and other equipment. The wind had picked up, and it railed against them, almost as if it meant to keep them inside. The feeling of the creeper following them returned not long into their walk. Ellen kept glancing back, thinking it was a real and alive person following them, but no visible person was there.

Mr. Murphy was already waiting for them in front of the stately manor, where his colonial bike leaned against an old whiskey barrel. Although he was wearing his colonial attire, his posture was different. He was no longer in character.

"Hey, ladies, thanks so much for meeting me here," he said in a voice unlike his previous one. It was a natural and modern-day voice.

"Thanks for inviting us," Ellen replied as she and her friends followed him up the sidewalk to the front door. "We brought along our equipment."

"And a few snacks," Sue added. "Are you hungry, Mr. Murphy?"

"Oh, call me Mark. And, yes, it's been a long day, and I'm starving."

Sue rummaged through her tote and brought out a box of crackers, which she handed to Mark.

"Wow. Thanks."

Jacinda opened the front door. Ellen wondered if she lived there.

"Come in," Jacinda welcomed them. "I just finished setting everything up."

They followed Jacinda up the stairs to the third floor. The old wooden steps groaned beneath their weight. The house felt nearly as chilly as the night outside, and there was something oppressive about it that made it difficult for Ellen to breathe.

Once they reached the third floor, they followed Jacinda down the hallway to the back of the house, to the oak-paneled bedroom where the white-capped ghost had confronted them the previous night. Lit candles lined the mantle over the fireplace, the nightstand near the four-poster bed, and a dressing table along the back wall. Two dining chairs and a stool had been placed in a circle with the two wingback chairs in front of the fireplace.

"Make yourselves comfortable." Jacinda waved toward the sitting area.

"Do you mind if we set up a few cameras?" Ellen asked.

Mark frowned as he finished chewing his cracker. "We really aren't supposed to allow recordings. Can we trust you not to post them online?"

"It's purely for the investigation," Sue assured him.

He glanced at Jacinda, who nodded.

"Alright, then," he said, before popping another cracker into his mouth.

Ellen and her friends positioned the three cameras in the room—one on the mantle, another on the dresser, and a third on the nightstand. Then, they took some initial readings of the electromagnetic frequencies and temperature.

"What kind of séance did you have in mind?" Tanya asked Mark. "Do you use a particular method?"

Mark glanced at Jacinda, who said, "We have a few flashlights set up in the room. And we ask the spirits to turn them on and off."

"They're just regular flashlights from Home Depot," Mark added. "And we ask for knocks. We really don't have special methods, I guess. Do you?"

Tanya nodded. "We've used the Ouija Board, pendulums, dousing rods, sketches, the ghost box, and a new method we learned recently called the Estes Method. But we've used knocks and other signs as well."

"Do you have luck with the flashlights?" Sue wondered.

"We do in this room," Jacinda replied. "Watch this." Then, in a louder voice, she asked, "Is anyone here with us from the beyond? If so, could you turn on one of the flashlights in the room?"

Within seconds, the light on the mantle turned on.

Ellen's mouth made a wide circle as she glanced at her friends. "Wow. That was quick."

"Now, can you turn it off?" Jacinda asked. "Just tap it again, and it will go off."

The light turned off.

Ellen flinched, not having expected the response to be immediate.

"Do you think that's Eve?" Tanya asked Jacinda.

The young woman nodded.

"Or, it could be Henry," Ellen pointed out since she still felt the creeper in the room with them.

"How would you feel about trying the Estes Method?" Sue asked them.

Mark shrugged. "How does it work?"

Ellen explained the method of depriving someone of sight and sound—except for the noise of the ghost box app—while another addressed the spirits.

"Oh, I like that," Mark said. "I've always been skeptical of the spirit box—or ghost box, as you call it. It always looks to me like investigators hear what they want to hear. But if the one listening to the radio frequencies can't hear the questions, well, that's interesting." He turned to Jacinda. "What do you think?"

"Let's give it a try."

"Great," Ellen said. "Who wants to go under."

"Tanya seems to be a good medium," Sue pointed out.

"But Jacinda has a solid connection with Eve," Mark argued. "Maybe she should be the conduit."

"It doesn't matter to me," Tanya said to Jacinda. "Be my guest."

Ellen handed her noise-cancelling headphones to the young woman. "You can plug them into my phone, since I already have the app." Ellen opened the app on her phone and handed it over. Then she brought out the blindfold.

"Can I sit down?" Jacinda asked.

"Of course," Ellen said. "We all can."

Sue took a wingback chair next to Jacinda. Ellen and Tanya each sat in a dining room chair, leaving the stool for Mark.

Once Jacinda was blindfolded and wearing the headphones, and the headphones were plugged into Ellen's phone, Ellen asked, "Can you hear me, Jacinda?"

When Jacinda made no reply, Sue said, "Okay, then. Let's begin."

"Leave," Jacinda said. "Danger."

"What's the danger?" Sue asked.

"Curse."

Sue raised her brows and glanced at Ellen and Tanya. "Who made the curse?"

"Indians."

"Indians cursed the house?" Sue asked.

"Yes," Jacinda replied. "Pow . . . uh . . . tan."

"I don't know what that means," Ellen whispered to Mark. "Do you?"

He shook his head. "Oh, maybe she's saying Powhatan Indians, or Chief Powhatan. That was Pocahontas's father."

"Yes," Jacinda said.

Ellen gasped. "Did Pocahontas's father curse this house?"

"Uh-huh," Jacinda said. "Right."

Ellen and her friends exchanged looks of surprise.

"Why?" Sue asked.

"Disturbed," Jacinda said. Then, after a beat, she added, "Graves."

"Someone disturbed Indian graves?" Sue asked.

"Yes. House."

Ellen snapped her fingers. "The building of this house disturbed the Indian graves, so the chief cursed it."

"Exactly," Jacinda said.

"Who are you?" Sue asked. "Can you tell us your name?"

Jacinda was quiet for a few moments. Just as Ellen was about to ask another question, the young woman said, "Eve."

Mark gasped. "It's really her."

"Danger," Jacinda said again. "I came here to help . . ."

"To help who?" Sue asked.

"My . . . son."

"Your son has moved on, Eve," Ellen said. "You can rest now."

"Trapped . . . we all are."

Tanya turned to Ellen. "Are multiple spirits trapped here?"

"Yes," Jacinda said. "Curse."

"Is your son with you?" Ellen asked.

"No."

"We give you permission to move on," Sue said. "Look for the light and go to the other side. Your son is waiting for you."

"Wait, can you do that?" Mark asked nervously.

"Cannot," Jacinda said.

"Is there a way to break the curse?" Ellen asked.

A few moments of silence passed before Jacinda said, "Medicine."

Ellen sucked in air. "Medicine?"

"What kind of medicine?" Sue asked.

"You know . . . spiritual."

Suddenly, all the candles on the mantle went out.

Ellen glanced around the room. "Eve, did you blow out the candles?"

"No."

A shiver rushed down Ellen's back. She felt stifled by negative energy.

"Is someone else here?" Sue asked.

"Many."

"Many other spirits are here?" Mark asked.

"Yes," Jacinda confirmed.

The candles on the dresser went out.

"That feels aggressive," Mark noted. "Maybe we should stop."

"Ow," Tanya cried. "Something scratched my ankle."

"We need to stop," Mark insisted again. "It can get ugly if we ignore the signs."

Sue tapped Jacinda on the shoulder. The young woman took off the blindfold and headphones.

"What was I talking about?" she asked.

Mark told her what had happened. Then he asked, "Do you know if Pocahontas's father was buried where this house now stands?"

"No, I don't."

Sue, who had already taken out her phone to search it up, said, "I found an article claiming that he and his daughter were both buried here, according to one of the previous owners—a Mrs. Graves. The article says that Mrs. Graves also claimed that the building of the Colonial National Historic Parkway tunnel beneath the house revealed that human remains had been buried on the east side of the estate, confirming what she'd always been told."

"How can we help Eve to move on?" Tanya wondered. "Is there a way to lift the curse?"

"If there is, I don't know what it is," Jacinda admitted. "We wouldn't want to further disturb any remains by digging them up."

"No, we wouldn't," Mark agreed. "And I'm not sure we should interfere with such things."

"Eve said it would take spiritual medicine," Ellen reminded them. "What could that mean?"

"Maybe we should ask a shaman," Sue suggested. "Why don't we call Mary Pullen for advice?"

"Great idea!" Ellen exclaimed.

Sue turned to Mark. "I get told that a lot, so you may as well get used to it."

Mark chuckled, but at the same moment, the stool beneath him broke, and he fell to the floor.

"Oh, my gawd!" Sue cried.

Tanya climbed to her feet and offered Mark her hand. "Are you okay?"

Ellen helped him climb to his feet.

"Let's get out of here," he said.

The young woman blew out the remaining candles. "Carry those chairs down for me, will you, Mark?"

As Ellen was about to descend the stairs, she felt something push against her. Another force in front of her prevented her from falling.

"Ellen?" Sue asked from behind her.

"Something pushed me!" Ellen cried. "And, well, I think something saved me, too."

"Be careful," Mark warned from behind her. "Hold onto the railing."

"How will you hold on with your hands full?" Sue asked the young man.

"I'll be careful," he promised.

Ellen was glad when they were finally out of Peyton Randolph House and back in the fresh night air. They waved goodbye to their tour guides and headed back to the Brick House Shop, the creeper following close behind.

"You are not allowed to follow us inside," Ellen said at the threshold once again, where she poured a line of protective salt.

"Do you really think that works?" Tanya asked.

"It doesn't hurt to try," Ellen replied as she hung up her coat on a hook in the entry. "I want to take a look at our footage."

The three friends sat together in the downstairs sitting room on the blue velvet couch looking at the monitor on their full spectrum camera. Ellen sat in the middle, operating the device. She slowed it down when she noticed several figures standing behind Jacinda.

Tanya gasped. "Oh, my gosh. Look at them all."

"I count at least thirteen," Sue reported.

"Did you get those three on the ceiling?" Ellen asked, pointing to the monitor as she paused it.

"Sixteen," Sue corrected herself. "And that's just what we're picking up in this shot. Who knows how many more of them were in the room."

Ellen bent over the bag at her feet and pulled out the other two cameras. As they scanned the other monitors, they couldn't believe what they saw. Some were stick figures, others were orbs, and still others were very transparent, nearly invisible apparitions.

"Poor things," Tanya cried, as she covered her mouth. "Dozens of trapped souls. They're crowded around us, probably hopeful for the first time in decades."

"We've got to help them," Sue declared. "I don't know how, but we've got to try."

CHAPTER ELEVEN

Crossings

On Monday, December twelfth, Ellen and her friends returned from San Antonio to Williamsburg for their ten-day holiday stay in Sue's finished vacation rental. This time, Ellen brought Moseby along—not because Brian couldn't watch him, but because she hated being away from him for very long.

They flew into Richmond, where a distant Frost relative of Ellen's met them at a sandwich shop near the airport. Her name was Brenda Hammond, and she was in her mid-seventies.

Brenda had already emailed Ellen part of the Frost family tree, but Brenda wanted to provide some details she knew in person.

"Your father was a World War II baby," Brenda said. "He was conceived while your grandfather was on leave, and, unfortunately, your grandfather died in the war and never met his son."

"Oh." Ellen's heart hurt for her father, who must have been sad to not have his father growing up.

"Your father was Frank, Jr., and his father was Frank, Sr. Frank, Sr. was a World War I baby. He also lost his father in war before he was born."

Although Ellen had been glad to meet a distant relative, especially one older than herself, someone who knew things about her family, the details of her line of the Frost family were depressing. She'd been hoping to feel a connection to Brenda, but whether it was the depressing details or something else, Ellen didn't feel it. Brenda felt like just another stranger to her.

Later, as they drove in their rental from the airport, her friends must have sensed her melancholy, because she could tell they were trying to brighten her mood.

"What are you most looking forward to in Williamsburg?" Tanya asked from the passenger's seat.

Sue, who was driving, said with a laugh, "Seeing the handsome Mr. Benson."

"Like mother, like daughter!" Tanya sang in a teasing tone.

"I can't wait to see Busch Gardens," Ellen said. "I need a Christmas pick-me-up."

Once they entered Williamsburg, Ellen noticed a candle in a window of nearly every home. Garlands and wreaths trimmed many a façade, and decorated Christmas trees could be seen inside shop windows along many of the streets.

Jason, Sue's contractor, met them at the house on Kestrel Court in the late afternoon for a final walk through. Ellen carried Mo in his cloth pooch carrier.

"It's perfect!" Sue ran her hands over the butcher block countertops. "Isn't it gorgeous?"

"It really is," Tanya agreed.

"I love that backsplash," Ellen said admiringly. "Everything goes together so nicely, especially the black iron fixtures, knobs, and pulls."

Sue put her hands on her hips. "I had a feeling that would be your favorite—either the metal finishes or the black front door."

"The door does look great," Ellen admitted.

"I can't wait to go shopping to help you fill this place up," Tanya said. "The new sofas you ordered look really nice in the two living areas, but you'll also need tables and lamps and wall art."

"And books for the library upstairs," Ellen added, "I've already ordered some written by my favorite authors."

"I need a dining table, too," Sue reminded them. "Though I did order a few things from Wayfair that should be arriving this week."

"We have quite a few antique stores here in Williamsburg," Jason mentioned. "I could text you the names of some of my favorites."

"The last time Sue went inside an antique store," Ellen began, "three people tried to buy her."

Sue chuckled. "And they were all men in their thirties who knew a good thing when they saw one."

"That's not what Tom says," Tanya teased.

"That's true," Sue joked. "He suffers daily from buyer's remorse."

Jason shook his head. "You ladies are something else."

Ellen turned to Jason. "Did you encounter anymore ghostly occurrences while you were finishing up?"

"A few—mostly the same things, you know. My tools kept disappearing on me. Drove me a little batty, but I handled it." Then he added, "It's too bad you can't ghost-proof the place."

Sue threw her hands up. "Well, I once tried to *child*proof my home, and that didn't go well. The kids still found a way in."

Jason laughed. Ellen and Tanya, having heard that joke before, exchanged grins.

Ellen followed Sue into the master suite, where a new king-size bed had replaced the old sleigh bed. This one had a gorgeous wooden headboard with three birds carved into it.

"It fits perfectly in here," Tanya admired.

"I feel like a kid in a candy store," Sue said. "It's all so exciting."

"I never had much willpower in a candy store," Ellen admitted as they took another look at the master bath.

Sue chuckled. "My mother used to say I had more *won't* power than *will* power."

Ellen smiled at Sue. "I miss her jokes. They were better than yours."

"Mom thought so, too," Sue said with a shrug. "Whenever she said so, I told her it was her dementia talking."

"That wasn't very nice," Tanya scoffed as they left the master suite.

"It was payback for a joke she used to say about *me* that wasn't very nice," Sue insisted.

Ellen paused in the family room. "Let's hear it."

Sue sighed. "How many Sues does it take to change a lightbulb?"

"How many?" Jason asked.

"One. Sue holds the bulb while the rest of the world revolves around her."

Ellen and Tanya guffawed.

Ellen slapped her knee. "I miss her so much!"

"Well, not more than I do," Sue stated.

Ellen put an arm around her friend. "The jury's still out on that."

"Are the other new beds already set up?" Tanya asked Jason as they headed for the stairs.

"Yes, ma'am."

They went upstairs to look at the new beds and to see the finished bathroom before heading back downstairs.

"We have our work cut out for us, ladies," Sue said when they reached the bottom floor.

"If you can really call shopping for home décor *work*," Tanya teased.

"We don't have to do it all in one day," Ellen pointed out. "I'm a little tired from the flight. Why don't we focus on the bedding and bedroom décor today and leave the rest for another day?"

"Sounds like a good plan," Sue agreed.

Sue wrote Jason his final check, and then they thanked him again at the front door.

"Best of luck with your ethereal guests," he said with a wave.

Ellen put Moseby on his leash and followed Jason down the front steps, so Mo could walk in the grass. She waved at the contractor as he drove away, and she breathed in the chilly air. Her mood had been lifted by her friends, by the house, and by Christmas. She returned indoors with a smile on her face.

Jason hadn't been gone ten minutes when Ellen and her friends heard water running in the kitchen. They rushed over to see steam rising from the sink and letters written in the condensation on the window: *GET OUT.*

Sue turned off the water. "Maybe this would be a good time to go shopping."

"Yes, let's," Tanya agreed.

Ellen scooped up Mo and returned him to his cloth pooch carrier. "I don't think I'll be leaving Moseby here alone."

They grabbed their coats and purses from the glass table in the breakfast nook and scurried out the front door.

Later that evening after a successful shopping trip and delicious meal at the Fat Canary, the three friends relaxed in the hot tub and drank frozen margaritas while Moseby lay curled on a rug in front of the cozy fireplace. The string of white outdoor lights lining the windows, along with a nearly full moon, illuminated some of the woods behind the house, which Ellen loved because it made her feel like they were in a treehouse.

"I adore the bedding we found at Macy's," Tanya said. "And it looks so nice on the beds."

"I still can't believe Ellen found that painting that goes so perfectly in my bedroom. It looks beautiful hanging over my bed."

"We lucked out with that big sale, didn't we?" Ellen said with a grin. "I think you saved a small fortune."

"If Tom asks, that's my story, and I'm sticking to it."

Ellen and Tanya giggled.

"I still don't understand why the ghosts in this house keep telling us to leave," Sue said after taking another sip from her drink. "Don't they want to cross over?"

"We've been told by other experts that not all do," Tanya reminded them, "and remember George Vanderbilt? He didn't want to move on but preferred to stay in his little piece of heaven. But I can't see why these poor families would want to remain in the place where they were murdered."

"I bet they want to move on," Ellen said before taking a sip of her margarita. "I think their warning has to do with Hamilton. They're looking out for us. Don't you think?"

"That makes sense," Tanya agreed.

Their anthropologist friend and his team had formulated a working list of names from both DNA evidence and the letters and other artifacts from the trunks. Bob had informed them that although the means for identifying the bodies required a degree of guesswork, thirty of the thirty-eight bodies were named, and four of the eight unnamed ones had been assigned surnames—they were children whose first names couldn't be deduced from the letters and journals. And there were four bodies for which neither DNA evidence nor information from the artifacts shed any light, except that they were related. Ellen and her friends planned to call out the names one by one and invite the ghosts to cross over to the other side.

Ellen hoped they could use their various investigative methods to learn the surname of the unidentified remains. They consisted of an adult male, an adult female, and two children—one male and one female. What made this family especially important to Ellen was that they were distant relatives of hers. Their DNA matched up with Ellen's father's Frost family bloodline.

"Does anyone want a second margarita?" Sue asked as she poured one for herself at a table next to the hot tub.

"I'd better not," Ellen said. "I need to keep my wits about me tonight."

Tanya handed her empty cup to Sue. "I'll take half of one. I need a little more courage."

As Ellen drank down the last of her margarita, her phone rang. She sat up and reached for it where it lay on a nearby end table.

"It's Mary Pullen," she said to her friends. Then, answering the phone, she said, "Hi, Mary."

"I finally found a local shaman for you," Mary began, "however, he says the medicine has to be spoken in the native Powhatan tongue to be really effective."

"Does he know how to speak it?" Ellen asked.

"He said it isn't spoken anymore. There's no remaining record of it—though scholars are trying to revive it. But he's willing to give the medicine a try if you are."

"Absolutely," Ellen said. "Can you text me his contact information?"

"Will do."

"Thank you, Mary."

Ellen relayed what Mary had said to her friends.

"It's certainly worth a shot," Sue said. "But I hope the Peyton Randolph House ghosts don't become our first failure."

Tanya climbed from the tub. "All we can do is try."

"Are you getting out?" Ellen asked Tanya.

"Yeah. I think I'll get dressed and start setting up."

Ellen didn't want to abandon Sue while her friend was finishing her second margarita. The cozy fire in the fireplace, Mo curled up on an area rug, the lights on the windows outside, and the hot, bubbly water soothing her bones and muscles were all rather heavenly to Ellen. She sat back in the corner of the tub and gazed at the trees. For a moment, she thought she saw the boy in the woods looking in at them again, but she may have been imagining it.

A little while later, Ellen sat in her pajamas across from Sue and Tanya lighting the candles in the center of their table, where they had also set a plate with different types of cheese, which they'd purchased earlier from the Cheese Shop. The Ouija Board and plastic planchette were there too, for when they asked the spirits to help them with the names. Tanya had created a circle of protection on the floor around them, and Ellen and Sue had set up their cameras and other equipment. Moseby lay asleep in front of the fire in the sunroom. Night had fallen, and the nearly full moon was partially visible in the clouds through the bay window beside her. Ellen and her friends were ready to begin.

"Should I read each name, one at a time?" Tanya held up the paper they'd received from Bob Brooks listing the probable names of the victims whose remains they'd discovered. She held a flashlight in the other, pointed at the document.

"Let's call to them first," Sue suggested. Then, in a louder voice, she said, "Spirits of the other realm, we've come to help you cross over to the other side, to find peace with your loved ones who have also passed away. Let us help you find comfort. To find us, look for the light of our candles. Smell the aroma of our food. Listen to the sound of my voice."

Ellen lifted her chin. "Any spirits with us tonight, we're sorry you've been trapped here, lost on this side. We believe you were scalped by Native Americans loyal to the British crown, under the orders of Lieutenant-Governor Henry Hamilton. Please know that you won't be forgotten for your sacrifice. You stood up for American freedom. We thank you for your sacrifice."

"You won't be forgotten," Sue echoed. "We're having a memorial made. Your names will be etched onto a sizeable boulder and placed in the front garden of this home, so you will never be forgotten."

One of the candles went out. Ellen relit it. "Lucy, is that you? If so, can you knock twice for yes? If that's not Lucy, please knock once."

They waited but heard no knocks. Then, there was a fluttering in the walls, like mice running through the drywalls again.

Ellen straightened her back. "Lucy? Is that you? If so, please give us a sign. You can knock twice or touch the device on the kitchen floor to make it beep twice."

The REM-POD beeped once.

The three friends jumped in their seats.

"Maybe it isn't Lucy," Tanya whispered.

"Lucy," Sue began, "if that's you, please touch the device twice. If that's not Lucy, then just touch it once."

One beep.

"Are we talking with Henry Hamilton?" Ellen asked. "If no, please touch the device once. If yes touch it twice."

One beep.

"Maybe we're talking to one of the other colonists," Tanya suggested. Then, more loudly, she asked, "Is Jane Barton here with us tonight? If so, can you make the device beep twice?"

Two beeps.

Tanya glanced excitedly at Ellen and Sue. "Are William Barton Senior, Joseph Barton, Constance Barton, and Francis Barton also present? If so, please touch the device twice."

Two beeps.

"That's awesome!" Ellen whispered.

"Barton family, look for the light on the other side," Sue instructed. "I call upon God's heavenly angels and any relatives of the Barton family, especially William Junior, to please open your arms and guide Jane, William Senior, Joseph, Constance, and Francis to the other side to find their everlasting peace."

Ellen repeated, "William Junior, along with God's angels, please welcome your family home."

There was another flutter in the walls, followed by a warm rush of air—so powerful that it blew Sue's hair about her face.

"What was that?" Ellen wondered.

"Maybe their souls flew past me," Sue speculated. "That's the feeling I got, anyway. Doesn't it seem lighter—the air, I mean?"

Ellen nodded. "And joyful, in a strange way."

"I feel it, too," Tanya mentioned. "I feel like I'm going to cry happy tears."

"Me, too." Sue's eyes were already welling with them.

Ellen wiped the tears forming in her own eyes. "Let's move on to the next family."

Tanya cleared her throat. "I'm calling on Justine, Adelaide, Timothy, Stephen, Ryan, and Elizabeth Cooper. Are you present? If so, please touch the device on the kitchen floor twice."

Ellen whispered, "This is the family the father sent paper to for making bonnets, remember?"

Her friends nodded as they waited for a sign. Tanya was about to repeat herself when she was interrupted by two beeps.

"Wonderful!" Sue cried.

"What a relief," Tanya said. "Suddenly, I was worried we had their names wrong."

"Cooper family," Sue began, "please look for the light on the other side. I pray to God's heavenly angels, along with any relatives already there, to guide you. Fly to the other side and find eternal rest."

"We are praying for you," Ellen added after a moment. "Look for God's heavenly angels to guide you. Justine, look for your husband. Cooper children, run to your father's open arms."

The pitter-patter in the walls was even louder this time—so loud, that Moseby came from where he'd been sleeping in the sunroom to see what was happening.

Then a rush of warm air pressed Ellen's hair away from her face. Pure joy entered her heart as tears flowed from her eyes. "This is so beautiful."

Moseby barked once.

"It's okay, Moseby-Mo," Ellen cooed with a laugh. "Go lay down."

He titled his head to the side and whined.

Worried that he might be frightened, Ellen quickly opened the circle, scooped him up, and closed it again. Then she sat down with him in her lap.

"Sorry about that," Ellen said to her friends. "Please continue."

Tanya squinted at the paper in her hand. "I'm so giddy with excitement that I can hardly see. Oh, here we go . . . Dickenson family—Marjory, Adam, Colin, Herbert, and Lucy. Are you here with us? If so, please touch the device on the kitchen floor twice."

They waited in silence. Mo squirmed in Ellen's lap.

"Dickensons?" Tanya repeated.

"My phone just died," Sue whispered.

Two of the three candles went out. Ellen quickly relit them.

The sound of water running made Ellen turn toward the kitchen sink, where steam began to rise from the basin. It was too dark to make out if anything was written on the window, so Tanya got up, opened the circle, and turned on the kitchen light.

Written in the condensation on the window were the words: *Sam is lost*.

Ellen immediately thought of the boy in the woods, who'd seemed to her to be about eleven or twelve years old with short brown hair.

Tanya turned to her friends. "What should we do?"

"Turn off the lights," Ellen replied. "I have an idea."

Tanya did as Ellen asked and returned to the circle, closing it behind her.

To the spirits, Ellen said, "Was Sam about eleven or twelve when he died? Please touch the device twice for yes and once for no."

Two beeps.

"Did he have brown hair?" Ellen asked. "Please—"

Two beeps.

"The boy in the woods," Ellen whispered.

"Why is he in the woods, though?" Tanya wondered. "You saw him right outside. How can he be lost?"

Sue touched her index finger to her chin. "I wonder if he got separated from the group. Maybe he ran off or was carried off."

"That's right," Ellen began. "Sam's name isn't listed, and if there had been another Dickenson, it would say *unknown Dickenson boy* like it says for the Smiths and Scammels."

"Exactly," Sue said. "This means that Sam's body is somewhere else."

"Lost in the woods," Tanya speculated.

"Maybe Sam can guide us to his remains," Ellen reasoned. "We could try with the dousing rods."

"Let's finish helping the rest of the spirits cross over," Sue suggested. "Then we can focus on Sam and the Dickenson family."

Tanya cleared her throat. "Phillips family. Are you here? Thomas, Wilma, Virginia, Alexander, and Spencer, if you're present with us tonight, please touch the device twice for yes."

Two beeps.

Tanya's brows lifted with surprise.

Sue smiled and Ellen sighed with relief.

Sue said, "Phillips family, please look for the light on the other side. I pray that God's heavenly angels and any relatives of yours will guide you with open arms to your eternal peace."

Another flutter sounded through the walls. Moseby lifted his head up and sat very still, listening, just as a woosh of warm air blew Tanya's hair into her face.

Tanya laughed and brushed it off with her fingers. "What a rush. We're making progress, ladies!"

"It's okay, Moseby-Mo," Ellen assured her dog. "Don't worry, sweet boy."

"Who's next?" Sue asked Tanya.

"Scammel family," Tanya announced. "James, Sarah, Alison, Hilary, Peter, Matthew, and two other Scammel children—one boy and one girl, are you here with us? If so—"

Two beeps.

"They seem anxious, don't they?" Ellen whispered.

"That's a good thing," Sue replied as she placed her fingers on the planchette of the Ouija Board.

Ellen and Tanya followed suit as Sue said, "Scammel family, please move this planchette to spell out the name of the boy whose name we did not say."

Ellen held her breath. For many seconds, the planchette didn't move.

"We can still help them move on," Tanya whispered, "even without the name."

"I want it for the memorial," Sue reminded her.

"Sarah Scammel," Ellen said. "You are the mother of Alison, Hilary, Matthew, and two other children. What are their names?"

The planchette began to move. It slowly crossed the board and stopped on J.

"J," Tanya whispered.

Then the planchette moved to A-C-O-B.

"Jacob," Tanya whispered.

"Sarah Scammel," Ellen called out. "Is Jacob the name of one of your sons? If so, make the device beep twice."

Two beeps.

"This so is great!" Tanya added Jacob's name to the list.

"Sarah Scammel," Ellen began again. "What is the name of your other child?"

The planchette moved to R-E-B-E-C-C-A.

"Rebecca," Tanya said before adding it to the list.

"Sarah Scammel," Ellen called. "Is Rebecca the name of one of your daughters? If so, please—"

Two beeps.

Then, Sue said, "Scammel family, please look for the light on the other side. I pray to God's heavenly angels and any Scammel relatives to please welcome your dearly departed with you to their heavenly peace."

The pitter-patter in the walls was loud, almost like a snare drum, and Mo jumped from Ellen's lap, destroying their circle of protection on the floor. Ellen snatched him up and returned to the table with her apologies to her friends just as a rush of warm air blew against her face. She closed her eyes and felt joy rush through her body.

"Wow," she said when it had finished, and she had opened her eyes. "That's such an amazing feeling."

"I know, right?" Tanya was giddy with laughter.

"Maybe you shouldn't have had that second margarita," Sue teased her.

"It's not the alcohol," Tanya insisted.

"I know," Sue assured her. "I feel as giddy as you. I can't believe this is happening."

"Let's move on to the other family," Ellen prompted. "I have a feeling they're anxious to go with their friends."

"Smith family?" Tanya called. "Lawrence, Josephine, Alma, Georgiana, and two other Smith children—two girls. Are you—"

Two beeps.

Ellen grinned. "I'm glad they're eager."

"They *have* been lost for over two hundred years," Tanya reminded her.

"We need the names of the two other girls," Sue announced.

When the planchette failed to move, Ellen called, "Josephine Smith, please use this planchette to spell the name of one of your daughters."

Once again, the planchette glided across the board. As it did, one of the candles went out.

The planchette spelled E-M-I-L-Y.

"Emily." Tanya added it to the list.

"Josephine Smith," Ellen began. "If Emily is the name of one of your daughters, please—"

Two beeps.

Ellen chuckled. "Okay then. Now, please spell out the name of your other—"

Before she could get the words out, the planchette began to move. This time it spelled out C-L-A-I-R-E.

"Claire." Tanya added it to the list.

Without Ellen having to ask, the REM-POD beeped twice.

"Very good," Ellen praised.

"Look for the light on the other side, Smith family," Sue instructed. "I pray to God's heavenly angels and to all the Smith relatives to please guide this lost family to the other side, where they can finally find everlasting rest."

The walls trembled and shuddered, and then a burst of warm air blew the hair of all three friends about their faces.

"That's thirty spirits saved," Tanya said with tears in her eyes. "We have the Dickensons and the unidentified family remaining."

Sue lifted her face toward the ceiling, "Spirits, we need help identifying some of you. There's one family whose surname we can't make out. Could you—"

Before Sue had finished her question, the planchette began to move. It spelled out F-R-O-S-T.

"Frost?" Ellen asked. "That's *my family*. Bob was right. Those are ancestors of mine."

Two beeps.

Tears filled Ellen's eyes. She shook her head, feeling silly. These ghosts weren't any closer to her than Brenda Hammond had been, biologically speaking, and yet she felt a connection to these spirits that was strong and comforting. Why should she feel close to ancestors she'd never heard of before? It made no sense. But her heart was filled with joy at knowing that she was in the same room with family members.

"Please spell out the name of the adult female," Tanya instructed.

The planchette spelled A-B-I-G-A-I-L.

"Abigail Frost?" Ellen asked.

Two beeps.

"Please tell us the name of the adult male," Tanya instructed.

The planchette moved to J-O-S-E-P-H.

"Joseph?" Ellen asked. Then she whispered to her friends, "That's Nolan's middle name."

Two beeps.

They did the same with the children and were given the name Harold for the boy and Harriet for the girl.

Tanya added the names to her list. "That's Abigail, Joseph, Harold, and Harriet Frost."

"Frost family," Ellen began, "*my family*, look for the light on the other side. I pray to God's heavenly angels and to the other members of our Frost family to welcome you to the other side, where you can finally enjoy eternal peace. Please say hello to my father, Frank, Jr. Please tell him how much I miss him."

The walls trembled again, and the warm air rushed by the back of Ellen's head and then blew Tanya's hair from her face.

"This is so incredibly satisfying!" Tanya cried gleefully.

Ellen felt a strange sensation—it wasn't physical, but she somehow felt it. It was almost as if her mind's eye perceived a bright orb fly from the ceiling in the corner of the family room and rush toward her. She jumped to her feet with Moseby in her arms and flailed backward when she lost her footing. Fortunately, she regained her balance and didn't fall with her sweet pup.

"Ellen?" Sue asked.

The orb vanished. Ellen shuddered and tried to snap back to reality as more tears filled her eyes. "I don't know how to explain it."

"Are you okay?" Tanya asked.

"More than okay," she said with a smile. "I think I just saw my father."

"Your father?" Sue repeated. "How do you know it was him?"

"I felt it. I don't know, I just felt it. But I'm sure."

"That's amazing." Tanya gave her a hug. "I'm so happy for you."

"Me, too." Sue said. "Jealous, but happy for you."

Still shaking, Ellen gently put Mo on the floor. "Let's go find Sam Dickenson."

CHAPTER TWELVE

Sam Dickenson

It was ten o'clock at night when Ellen and her friends put on their coats and boots and headed outside, where it had begun to snow. Sue walked Moseby on his leash so Ellen could use the dousing rods. Tanya carried one of the full-spectrum cameras to record their attempt to find Sam Dickenson in the woods.

Once they were behind the house, Ellen cried out, "Sam Dickenson, I'm here to help you find your family. Your parents and sister, Lucy, and brother . . ." Ellen turned to Tanya, "What was his name?"

"Herbert," Tanya answered.

"Your sister, Lucy, and brother, Herbert, want to find you," Ellen said. "Can you guide us to where your body lies in the earth? Use these rods I'm holding. If I'm going the right way, push the rods together. If I'm going the wrong way, push them apart. If you can hear me and you agree, push them apart."

The wind was blowing, causing the rods to move back and forth in Ellen's hands. There was no way to steady them.

"This isn't going to work," Sue pointed out. "We need a better method."

Ellen sighed with frustration. Sue was right.

"The EMF detector," Tanya suggested. "You can ask him to touch it when you're going the right way and to move away from it when you're going the wrong way."

"Good thinking, Tanya!" Ellen hurried inside the house and exchanged the rods for the EMF detector. Once she was back outside with her friends, she said, "Sam? If you're here, please come and touch this box in my hand. If you do, it will flash, letting me know you're here."

Ellen and her friends huddled together, staring at the instrument. The small bulbs on the device did not light up. Moseby began to whine.

"Maybe I should take him back indoors," Sue said of the dog.

"I don't want him left alone," Ellen said. "Would you mind carrying him? He might just be cold."

Sue bent over and scooped him up. "Maybe we can keep each other warm. Right, boy?"

"Sam?" Ellen called again. "I promise it won't hurt if you touch this box. It will measure your energy and let me know you're there, even if I can't see you. Of course, if you want to appear to me as you have in the past, please do!"

"It flashed red!" Tanya cried. "It's not doing it anymore, but he's here! I can see the stick figure of a child."

Ellen stared at the instrument. A few seconds later, it flashed from white to red.

"I hope that's him," Ellen muttered. "There's nothing else that could cause that, is there? We aren't around any electrical wires or anything."

"It's something supernatural," Sue said. "I can feel it."

Ellen wished she had worn gloves. Her hands were freezing. "Sam, if that's you, could you guide me toward the place where your body lies? If I'm going the right way, touch this box. If I'm going the wrong way, move away from it. It's like a game. Your mom and dad and sister and brother want you to play it to help me find you."

Ellen stepped further into the woods, toward the place where she had first spotted the boy. She and Tanya shined their lights on the ground. Even with a full moon, the canopy of trees made it difficult to see.

The EMF detector flashed orange and then red.

"You're going the right way," Tanya, recording beside her, said. "Sometimes the camera picks him up, but not always. It's picking him up now."

The instrument continued to flash between orange and red as they walked deeper into the woods, past the rows of birch trees and into thicker brush. They pressed bushy branches out of their way and soon came upon a dry creek bed. The instrument stopped flashing.

Ellen turned to the left and took a few steps, but the EMF detector didn't respond.

"The camera isn't picking him up," Tanya lamented.

"Try going the other way," Sue advised.

Ellen turned the other way and took a few steps. Her device began to flash again. "This way!"

She followed the creek bed for another five yards but stopped when the device stopped flashing. She took a few steps to her right, and the instrument didn't respond—nor did it respond when she moved to the left. She backtracked a few steps, and it flashed again.

"I think this is the spot," Ellen said excitedly. "Sam, if your body is lying in the ground beneath my feet, please touch this device once more."

Immediately, it flashed to red.

"The camera is picking him up again!" Tanya cried.

"We need to call Bob Brooks in the morning," Sue said. "We're not digging up another body."

"That's funny," Tanya began, "I don't recall you doing a lot of digging."

"Even so, it was enough."

Ellen pulled out her phone. "I'm calling him now. Hopefully he can jump on the first available flight."

She entered his number.

"Merry Christmas," Bob said by way of greeting.

"Merry Christmas, Bob. How soon can you come to Williamsburg? We found another body, another Dickenson boy."

"Another body? Where is it? What kind of shape is it in? How do you know it's a Dickenson boy?"

"Well, we haven't actually dug it up yet, but we know where it is and who it is, so when can you and your team get here?"

"Ellen, it's Christmas break. My students have gone home for the holidays. *I've* gone home for the holidays."

Ellen gave her friends a worried glance. "Then, what are we supposed to do?"

"Wait until January. I can come right after the new year."

"Bob, that's not soon enough. The family is waiting to move on."

"They've waited for over two hundred years. They can wait a few more weeks."

"Okay, Bob. Happy Holidays." Ellen hung up the phone and turned to her friends. "We're on our own."

An hour later, Ellen sat in an armchair in the sunroom with Moseby curled in her lap. They sat before a cozy fire—still burning because she had just fed it a new log. Her friends had gone to bed, but Ellen was too distracted to sleep. She felt as if she'd let the Dickenson family down by not helping them to cross over with the others tonight.

It must have been agonizing for them to have no idea where Sam was all these years, and for him to be alone and lost from the others. Ironically, he was so close. So close! Tonight, she had tried to coax him back to the house, telling him his family was waiting for him, but later, when she and her friends had questioned the spirits, they had said that Sam was nowhere to be found.

Why had he been unwilling or unable to follow?

Gazing at the falling snow through the windows of the sunroom, she wondered if his hesitance had anything to do with the creeper that seemed to be constantly at her side.

"Oh, Henry," she began, just above a whisper, "what on earth do you want from me?"

The log in the fireplace shifted. Ellen jumped up with Mo in her arms to investigate. It seemed to be nothing—just the resettling of the log after part of it had burned.

As she returned to her chair, she stopped short when she saw something in the window. Standing on the edge of the woods between two birch trees was the boy ghost she believed to be Sam. He stood there, staring at her, and she stood, staring back.

"Moseby," Ellen whispered. "Do you want to go outside?"

He licked her nose and wiggled his consent. She put on her boots, found her coat and his leash, and together they took the stairs from the sunroom to the woods. The whole while, the apparition of the boy remained visible.

When she and Moseby were only a few yards away from the boy, the ghostly figure pointed to the sky. Ellen looked up to find the moon was full and free of any cloud covering, and its light illuminated the snow-covered ground. The snow wasn't thick, but it was enough to brighten the night on the edge of the woods.

"You can show yourself when the moon is full?" Ellen asked.

The boy nodded. Then, he asked in a voice that was barely audible, "Can I pet your dog?"

As much as Ellen wanted to say yes, she was frightened for Moseby. "I don't know if he'll like that. He's afraid of strangers."

The boy hung his head.

"Why won't you follow me into the house and join your parents and siblings?"

"I can't." Transparent tears welled in his transparent eyes.

"Why not?"

He rubbed his eyes. "I'm too ashamed."

Ellen lifted her brows. She hadn't seen this coming. "I don't understand what you could possibly be so ashamed of that it would keep you away from your family."

"I ran when the Injuns came," he blubbered through his sobs. "I followed 'em here and watched." He heaved a few more sobs. "I didn't try an' stop 'em. I could've done something an' I didn't."

Ellen knelt in the snow beside Moseby, who was beginning to whine. As she stroked Mo's fur, she said, "Sweet boy, there's nothing you could have done to stop what happened."

He shook his head. "I'm a coward."

"You're a young boy."

"I could've run for help. I could've thrown rocks. I could've snuck up on the chief and slit his throat with my pocketknife. I've spent a long time thinking about what I could've done instead of hiding in the woods like a fool watching my family and friends get scalped."

"I promise there wasn't anything you could have done to change that, Sam. I doubt there was time to go for help. And, had you, you would have likely added to the death toll. And do you really believe throwing rocks would have solved anything? Or sneaking up on them? They had bows and arrows and were grown men."

"Not that grown. Some of 'em were young."

"You were outnumbered though, right?"

The boy nodded.

"Your parents and Lucy and Herbert love you and miss you."

The boy fell to his knees, covered his face, and sobbed. "I left 'em. I didn't do anything to help 'em. I hate myself."

Moseby whined.

Ellen scooped up Moseby and moved on her knees closer to the apparition. "Maybe he'll let you pet him if I hold him."

The boy wiped his eyes and crawled toward her in the snow. Then he patted Moseby's head and smiled.

"I always liked dogs."

"I think he likes you, too," Ellen said as she stroked Mo's fur, relieved that he wasn't barking or whining.

"What's his name?"

"Moseby. Sometimes I call him Mo, or Moseby-Mo."

"He's cute. Where did you get him?"

"He was lost, just like you."

"I'm not lost. I know exactly where I am."

Ellen lifted her brows again. "Well, your family thinks you're lost."

"They do? Are they still at the house?"

"Yes, and they're worried about you."

"I thought they'd gone to heaven already."

"No. They've been waiting for you. They want you to go with them to the other side, to find peace. It will be better than reliving your regret day after day."

"I don't deserve it." He started to cry again.

"Of course, you do. You did nothing wrong. Any parent would agree. They wanted you to run. If I had been your mother, I would have been happy that you ran."

"Really?" He patted Mo on the head again.

"Absolutely."

"You think my mom feels the same?"

"I know she does." Ellen tilted her head to the side. "Would you mind telling me how you died?"

"The Injuns heard me crying in the woods. They found me and raised their tomahawks. That's all I remember."

Ellen shuddered. "Will you follow me to the house to be reunited with your family?"

He fought against his sobs. "I want to, but I'm afraid. I don't think they love me anymore."

Ellen was so saddened by his words that she, too, began to cry. "Sam, they never stopped. They've been waiting for you all these years. They won't move on without you."

"They won't? They really won't?"

Ellen shook her head and stood up. "I tried to get them to go, and they refused to leave you."

"They did?"

Ellen was moved by how surprised the boy was to learn that his family would not leave this plane without him. She held out a shaky hand. "Come on, Sam. They're waiting for you."

The ghost boy put his transparent little hand into hers. She could barely feel it. It felt like a cold draft against her skin. She carried Mo in the crook of her other arm as she climbed up the sunroom steps and into the house. As they entered the family room, the flutter in the walls shook the house. The kitchen sink turned on, and steam rose from the basin. Ellen turned on the kitchen light just as Sue entered from the master suite.

"Ellen?" She rubbed her sleepy eyes. "Everything okay?"

"Sam's here." Ellen glanced at the apparition beside her. It was so faint that she could barely see it anymore.

"How did you manage that?"

Ellen grinned. "I've got skills, girlfriend."

Tanya approached from the stairs, squinting against the light from the kitchen. "What's happening?"

"Sam followed me home," Ellen explained. "He's ready to be reunited with his family."

Ellen could no longer feel his hand. She looked down, and he'd disappeared. "At least, I think he's here."

She turned off the water at the sink. In the condensation on the window were the words, *Thank you*.

"Yes, he's here." Ellen pointed to the window as more tears slid down her cheeks. "Now, let's help them cross over."

Tanya and Sue joined Ellen and Moseby at the table, where Ellen relit the candles.

Then Tanya read from the list, "Dickenson family—Marjory, Adam, Collin, Herbert, Lucy, and . . . Sam." Tanya quickly added Sam's name to the document. "Are you here with us? If so, please touch the device on the kitchen floor twice."

Two beeps.

Ellen smiled as gratitude swept over her.

Sue cleared her throat. "Dickenson family, please look for the light on the other side. I pray to God's heavenly angels and to any Dickenson relatives to please help guide you over to your eternal rest."

"We pray for your everlasting peace," Ellen added, unable to hold back her tears.

The walls shook, as if an earthquake were unsettling Williamsburg. Then, a rush of warm air whirled around the three friends, extinguishing their candles. Ellen was filled with the most profound joy as she gazed up and tears streamed from her eyes. With her mind's eye, she could see Sam flying with his family toward heaven.

Ellen looked at her friends and saw that they were crying, too.

Sue wiped her cheeks. "It never does get old, does it?"

"Congratulations on another job well done," Ellen said with a smile.

"Not completely done," Tanya pointed out. "We still have to figure out what to do with our creeper."

CHAPTER THIRTEEN

The Busch Gardens Incident

Ellen, Sue, and Tanya spent a lazy Tuesday morning recovering from their emotionally charged night. Most of Ellen's books had arrived, and she enjoyed unboxing them and organizing them on the built-in shelves upstairs. The house felt lighter with its previous tenants finally free from their trap of over two hundred years. And, although Ellen and her friends could still sense the presence of the creeper, he seemed more of a nuisance now than a threat. Even so, they were determined to get to the bottom of why he was there, but not without enjoying their holiday vacation. Since it was supposed to rain later in the week, they decided to spend the day at Busch Gardens.

In the late afternoon, after arranging the tables and area rugs that had arrived from Wayfair, Ellen and her friends bundled up in their coats and hats and took Moseby in their rental car, excited to see Christmas Town with its more than ten million twinkling lights. The snow had melted, and it was a beautiful day in the thirties without a cloud in the sky. They spent less than ten minutes waiting in line at the entrance, and then they arrived at an area named "England."

Sue pulled up the app on her phone. "The first show we want to catch is right here."

Just then, a group of Christmas carolers wearing Victorian coats and hats began to sing "We Wish You a Merry Christmas" in front of a clock tower. Ellen and her friends stopped to listen before heading into the Globe Theatre to watch the Christmas musical, *Scrooge No More*, which was based on the classic *A Christmas Carol*, by Charles Dickens.

After a delightful, hour-long production, Ellen and her friends walked with Moseby to "Scotland" to see the Clydesdale horses. Upon their arrival, one of the horses shrieked and reared back. The stable manager quickly jumped into the enclosure to calm the animal down.

"Was it my dog?" Ellen wondered as she hugged Moseby in his cloth pooch carrier.

"Dogs don't usually spook her," the stable manager replied. "I don't know what's gotten into her."

"It's our creeper," Sue declared with a frown.

Tanya complained to the air behind them, "Why can't you leave us alone?"

An older man a few yards away, muttered, "Pardon me," before turning in the opposite direction.

Tanya's face turned the color of raspberries as Sue giggled and Ellen covered her mouth. People were staring at them.

They quickly rushed inside a shop, where Ellen bought plush sheep toys for her grandbabies. Sue thought they were so cute that she got one for her grandbaby, too.

"I wonder if I'll ever have grandchildren," Tanya complained with a sigh. "I'm so jealous. I want to buy cute gifts, too."

"Buy them for your kids," Sue said. "I bet Cammie would love this T-shirt."

She held up a shirt with a sexy man wearing a kilt with text that read, "Balls like these don't fit in trousers."

Ellen busted out laughing.

"She probably *would* like that," Tanya admitted as she took the shirt from Sue.

"Besides," Ellen added, "you will have grandkids. It's just a matter of time."

"Hopefully I'll be around for them."

"You will," Sue assured her. "A lot can happen in a single year."

From the shop, the three friends hopped on the Christmas Town Express. The train provided them with a leisurely and scenic ride winding past snowy embankments and twinkling blue lights that made a breathtaking waterfall effect, especially now that dusk had fallen. Positioned in front of this incredible light display were life-size polar bears. Just past the bears, the train rounded a corner and entered "Italy," where they were greeted by a brightly lit Christmas tree on their right and a snowy path of grazing, life-size reindeer on their left—one of which had a bright, red nose.

"Look, Sue," Ellen pointed past the reindeer to a behemoth of a ride called "Apollo's Chariot." "Isn't that the rollercoaster you wanted to ride?"

"That's exactly why I came—to be jerked around and frightened within an inch of my life."

"What about that one?" Tanya pointed to another rollercoaster called "The Pantheon."

"I think Italy's too exciting for us," Sue said as they crossed a bridge over an artificial river that ran through the park. "Now, Germany looks more like our speed. I see a sign for beer and pretzels, and I think we should head that way."

Although there were Christmas trees throughout the gardens—some illuminated and others dusted with snow—the tree in "Germany" was the pièce de résistance of Christmas trees. At least fifty feet tall and covered with hundreds of lights and ornaments, it was a spectacular sight to behold. The three friends exited the train station and stood before the tree in awe while "villagers" sang "O Tannenbaum."

"It really is beautiful," Sue said admiringly. "I wish now I would have come with my mother when she was alive."

Ellen put an arm around her friend's shoulders. "I'm sure she thought of you, too, whenever she stood here."

Tanya, who stood on the other side of Sue, wrapped her arm around Sue's waist. "I'm so lucky to have you two as my friends."

"You really are," Sue teased with a sniffle.

Tanya chuckled. "I'm starving. Where are the beer and pretzels you were talking about?"

Next to the enormous tree was the Brauhaus Craft Bier Room where Ellen and her friends ate Rueben sandwiches and giant pretzels and drank steins of delicious, cold beer. Moseby enjoyed snacking on some of Ellen's sandwich.

They ate and visited until it was time to see the next show—*Up on the Haustop*, in Das Festhuas, next door to the restaurant. Ellen thought the singing was exceptional, and the performers sang many of her favorites, like "The Little Drummer Boy" and "Deck the Halls."

Mo was being such a good boy. He was rewarded with a walk after the show through the North Pole.

Night had fallen when they walked beneath an enormous, light-covered trellis with candy canes, ribbon, and poinsettias. Once through the trellis, they entered a cute German shop where they were offered two red, robust wines for sampling. They each bought a bottle, along with a few more gifts for their loved ones. They even found a gorgeous wreath for Sue's front door.

As they passed by Santa's Workshop, Sue, who had pulled out her phone to look at her app, said, "I think we should take the Sky Ride to France, if we want to make it in time for the last showing of *'Twas that Night on Ice*. It's rather a long walk. Otherwise, and we might not make it. Does that sound okay to y'all?"

"The Sky Ride only goes one-way, in the opposite direction," Ellen pointed out. "I suppose we can ride it to England and then take it to France from there."

"I think that will be quicker than walking," Sue argued.

"Sounds fun to me," Tanya replied. "I bet the view will be stunning from up there."

Tanya had been right. The sparkling river reflected the lights as it flowed through snowy embankments that were lined with polar bears and reindeer and real Clydesdales. As they flew over "Ireland," they also saw real black-face sheep, highland cattle, gray wolves, and eagles. The animals, along with the twinkling Christmas trees, ribboned wreaths, giant candy canes and peppermints, and other holiday décor, made for a breathtaking view. Even Moseby stretched from his carrier to check out the sights, wagging his tail with glee.

The ice show at the Royal Palace Theatre in "France" was a delight. Ellen and her friends kept warm in the outdoor theatre with hot cups of cocoa. After the show, they sampled smooth, white wine at the nearby La Belle Wine Bar and couldn't resist buying a bottle each. Then they checked out the pottery shop and the General Store before catching the Christmas Town Express back to "Scotland." The train afforded a view of the park that wasn't accessible elsewhere, as it wrapped through a snow-covered forest of twinkling Christmas trees. From the train station in "Scotland," they walked past the Clydesdales and over a bridge into "Ireland."

They had a half-hour to kill before their next show, so they watched the riders on a giant swinging ride, called "Finnegan's Flyer," before they meandered into a castle where Santa was performing his fireside chat with Mrs. Claus and a party of elves. Families dined at tables beside the stage. Ellen thought it would be fun to come back with her grandkids one day.

Ten minutes before the next show was to begin, Ellen and her friends filed into the Abbey Stone Theatre, wishing they'd arrived earlier, as it was packed. Once the *Celtic Fyre Christmas Celebration* began, they quickly saw why. The Irish cloggers performed the best show yet. The spirited ensemble danced and sang hilarious lyrics that had the three friends in stitches.

The half hour went by fast, and they were still laughing as they left the theatre.

Tanya clapped her hands. "That was so good. This has been such a fun day, even if you-know-who hasn't left our side once."

"I wonder if he enjoyed the show, too," Ellen said.

Sue took out her phone. "There's one more show that I want to see, but it's all the way over in Italy, and it starts in twenty minutes."

"Can we make it?" Tanya wondered. "I'm getting tired, to tell you the truth."

Sue put her hands on her hips. "I think if we hop on the train in Scotland and get off in Germany, we can cross a bridge and be right there."

"Let's do it," Ellen said enthusiastically.

The thirty-minute musical celebrating the nativity in an outdoor theater was lovely, but by the end of it, Ellen and her friends were ready to leave. Even Moseby was tired, having fallen asleep in his cloth pooch carrier. They decided to catch the Sky Ride in "Germany" for a scenic route back to the front entrance.

While they were in the air over the sparkling river and twinkling lights, the carriage they were in suddenly stopped.

"What's going on?" Tanya wondered as all three of them glanced around.

Then the carriage began to swing.

"Why is this happening?" Sue said nervously. "There's no wind."

Mo whimpered.

"It's okay, boy," Ellen cooed, even though her heart was racing.

The swinging carriage came to standstill, but then it jolted abruptly in a series of starts and stops.

Tanya, her face stricken with terror, clung to the carriage and screamed. "Help!"

People on the ground below stopped and looked up at them. Some of them pointed.

Ellen turned to see that another carriage was headed directly for them. If they collided, would the carriages fall fifty feet to the ground?

"Is this really happening?" Sue groaned.

Hugging Mo close, Ellen said, "If this is it, I just want y'all to know I love you guys."

"Don't talk like that," Sue said nervously. "This can't be it. I'm not ready to die."

"Oh, God, oh, God, oh, God," Tanya prayed. "Please don't let this be it."

Ellen glanced up at the full moon and said a silent prayer before she closed her eyes and gave in to God's will. *Whatever happens, happens,* she thought with resignation. *I've had a good life, and I'm grateful.*

Despite Tanya's screams, thoughts of seeing Paul again comforted Ellen as she held her breath and waited for the inevitable crash.

When no crash came, she opened her eyes to find the carriage illuminated with light. They were moving now with the second carriage close behind them. Ellen blinked at the vision in the center of the light. It was a dark face with red eyes.

"Help," he began. "You."

"You helped us?" Sue asked.

"Listen," he said. He was trying frantically to speak but only about every few words were audible. "I . . . you."

Ellen stroked Mo, who continued to whimper. "Are you Henry Hamilton?"

"Yes."

"And you want our help?" Sue asked through trembling lips.

"No!"

His answer came loudly and was delivered with so much force that the carriage swung side to side again.

Tanya, whose arms were shaking so badly that they appeared to be flapping like wings, asked, "You want to help *us*?"

"Yes!"

The carriage swung again, hard, and jerked forward and back.

The bright light vanished and the scary face with it, and the carriage neared the exit. Ellen hugged the attendant who opened their carriage door. Then, she and her friends walked on shaky limbs and caught their breath as they processed what had just happened.

"Did he cause that, or did he save us?" Tanya wondered.

"I don't know," Sue said. "I'm just glad to be alive."

Ellen hugged her precious Moseby close to her. "I think the creeper caused it."

"You do?" Tanya asked.

Ellen nodded. "Let's get home and use our equipment to talk to him. Let's find out what the hell he wants and get him off our backs."

"He says he wants to help *us*," Sue pointed out. "Help us how?"

Tanya led the way from the park. "Hopefully, we'll find out tonight."

CHAPTER FOURTEEN

The Monster

As soon as they returned to the house on Kestrel Court, Ellen and her friends put their shopping bags in a corner of the formal living room, removed their coats and boots, and prepared to communicate with Henry. Ellen took a moment away from her preparations to feed and water Moseby in the kitchen, and while he ate, she made a cozy fire in the family room. By the time he'd finished eating, the fire was burning. She called him to the couch and told him to lay down, and then she returned to the breakfast nook and sat with her back to the kitchen, so she could keep an eye on her pup.

Tanya lit the candles in the center of the table.

"Are you going under again?" Sue asked her.

"Would you mind doing it this time?" Tanya asked. "I'm not feeling it tonight. I'm still freaked out."

"I could do it," Ellen offered, though she really didn't want to, either.

Sue took up the headphones and blindfold. "I don't mind." She put on the headphones and blindfold. "Ready."

"You sure you can't hear us?" Ellen tested.

No reply.

"Good," Ellen said. Then, more loudly, she announced, "Henry Hamilton? You've been following us since the day we arrived but have so far been unable to communicate your message. We have devices here with us that can help. Use the ghost app connected to the headset to choose words in response to our questions. If you can't do that, you can always knock, make the lights flicker, or show some other sign. We have another device on the kitchen floor called a REM-POD. All you have to do is touch it to make it beep. Having said all that, I ask you now to give us a sign that you're here."

The lights in the kitchen, which had been turned off, flickered on and off again.

Tanya's brows shot up.

"Henry," Ellen began, "can you confirm that that was you who made the lights flicker by doing it again?"

The lights flickered again.

"Perfect," Tanya said beneath her breath. "He's here."

"Henry, the lights will only allow us to ask you yes and no answers," Ellen explained. "To give us your message, it would be more effective if you could communicate through our friend, who is waiting for you to select words from many radio broadcasts."

In the next instant, Sue's head began to bob. "I've been waiting for you to invite me in again for months."

"Sue?" Ellen climbed to her feet.

"I shall only use your friend for the time it takes to deliver my message," Sue said in a voice that was hers but not hers.

"Don't hurt her," Tanya demanded. "You aren't allowed to possess her."

"Did you cause that near-disaster during our sky ride?"

"You ladies are bloody exasperating," he said through Sue. "I could think of no other way to get your attention."

"Can't you make yourself appear to us in the full moon?" Ellen asked. "One of your victims was able to. We helped him cross over."

"I know. And yes. But it would only frighten you."

"We've seen a lot of ghosts," Ellen assured him.

"My shame, my guilt, my despair . . . have twisted my soul. My appearance is . . . monstrous."

Ellen shuddered, recalling the dark face and red eyes she had seen in their carriage.

"I can help you. If you agree to help me."

"Help us how?" Ellen sat back down.

"Break the curse at Peyton Randolph House. I heard what Eve said. You need spiritual medicine. I also heard what your shaman friend told you. The medicine must be spoken in Powhatan, which I happen to know."

"You know how to speak it?" Tanya asked.

"Yes," Henry confirmed as Sue's head continued to bob. "Bring your medicine man, and I'll help, if you help me."

Ellen gave Tanya a worried glance. "What do you want from us?"

"There are more," Henry said through Sue.

"More what?" Tanya wanted to know.

"Lost souls . . . because of me."

Ellen and Tanya exchanged looks of confusion.

"Do you mean to say there are more lost families, like the ones that haunted this house?"

"Like Lucy, yes—scalped by Indians and left to die in mass graves."

Ellen's mouth dropped open. "How many? Where?"

"Twenty-six in Colby Swamp and forty-three in Jolly Pond. Go to Freedom Park tomorrow at dusk, and I will show you where to find those in Colby Swamp. Tomorrow, at dusk, I will lead you to those in Jolly Pond."

"How?" Tanya asked.

"Meet me at the pond's southernmost point near the road," he replied through Sue. "But tonight, we begin at Freedom Park."

Ellen and Tanya gazed at one another wearing similar looks of amazement.

Sue's head slumped forward. Tanya and Ellen jumped to their feet and removed the headphones and blindfold.

Sue blinked and looked up at them. "What happened? Did I fall asleep?"

The next morning, after breakfast at Aromas in Colonial Williamsburg and a quick purchase of more chocolates from Wythe Candy and Gourmet Shop, Ellen and her friends and Moseby were walking through Merchant's Square when they passed Mark Murphy in his colonial attire riding his colonial bike. He waved and circled back over to them.

"Good morning, ladies. How are you on this fine day?" He dismounted his bike and walked beside them through the square.

It was cloudy and sprinkling, but Ellen supposed, all in all, it was a fine day. "Very well. How are you?" Mo tried to run between Mark's legs, but Ellen stopped him with the leash.

Mark tipped his colonial hat. "Fine, thank you. What a cute dog. What's his name?"

"This is Moseby," Ellen replied.

"In addition to being a bellhop, historian, and actor, I'm also a huge fan of dogs. May I pet him, or is he working?"

"You can pet him."

Ellen stopped walking to hold Moseby in place while Mark Murphy ran his fingers through Mo's fur.

"He is a sweet thing, is he not?"

"He is," Ellen agreed.

"We have news," Sue said eagerly as they continued walking.

"Good news, I hope," Mr. Murphy stated.

Ellen and her friends told him what they had learned from the ghost of Henry Hamilton.

"You really think you can break the curse?" Mark asked with a frown and in a more natural voice than he had used thus far.

"We hope so," Tanya piped up. "Don't you? You look concerned."

"Well, the ghosts are part of the home's charm. I would hate to lose them."

Ellen widened her eyes. "Don't you want them to find peace?"

"Yes, of course, of course."

For an actor, he wasn't very convincing.

Then he murmured, "I wonder how the board will feel about this. We need colonists in Colonial Williamsburg."

"Surely, there are enough who want to be here," Ellen began, "that you can do without those who don't."

"I suppose that is true, dear madam," Mark said, returning to character. "But I would think you will need permission to perform a ritual in Peyton Randolph House, especially if you plan to bring a medicine man to help you."

"Can't you help us with that?" Sue wondered.

"Have you already secured your medicine man?"

"We have a meeting scheduled with him tomorrow," Tanya explained.

"Let us reconvene at Peyton Randolph House tonight after my last tour to discuss this. Around ten o'clock? Perhaps we can ask the ghosts how they really feel about it."

"I don't know." Ellen guided Moseby on his leash away from a piece of trash. "We told Henry we'd go to Freedom Park tonight at dusk."

Mark Murphy hopped on his bike. "Meet me at the house afterward. I bid you farewell until then, ladies."

He rode away without their reply.

Ellen and her friends arrived in their rental car at Freedom Park just before dusk. Moseby was excited to be on leash in a new place and was ready to explore. Ellen was feeling apprehensive as she and Sue and Tanya each grabbed a map at the Welcome Center and walked over to what was marked as one of America's first free black settlements.

Although Ellen wanted to tour the three historical cabins and surrounding gardens, they needed to find Colby Swamp before dark.

"It looks like we want trail number three," Sue, looking up from her map, said. "Thank goodness it's paved. My feet are killing me today."

"Probably from all that walking we did at Busch Gardens," Tanya guessed.

"I think it was today's shopping at the outlet mall that did it," Sue admitted.

It was still sprinkling as they found the trailhead and followed it past the botanical gardens and an eighteenth-century cemetery into thickly forested pines and birches. Moseby kept wanting to stop to sniff everything, but Ellen urged him to keep up the pace. Along the way, Ellen noticed other trails, that weren't paved, winding through the woods. According to her map, there were trails for motor biking and regular biking that weren't in use due to the weather. In the distance, Ellen spotted two deer. Mo, spotting them too, stopped. Ellen gently pulled his leash to get him to continue.

Ellen noticed that they were the only people out at the park this late, and she began to wonder how smart it was for them to be there alone with a ghost that had admitted that he'd become a monster. Why should they trust him? What if he wasn't leading them to a mass grave but was instead planning to make a mass grave out of them?

After about a half-mile, they came up to a bridge which, according to the map, crossed over Colby Swamp.

"Okay, Henry," Sue, panting, announced. "Now what?"

Ellen noticed that on the right side of the bridge, the swamp was shallow, and there was a manmade dam, along with fallen logs where two beavers were furiously working on their own little dam. On the left side of the bridge, the swamp was dry. It was just a field of tall grass illuminated by the nearly full moon that had finally come out from behind the clouds.

"At least it finally stopped sprinkling," Tanya said. "The rain makes it feel so much colder than it really is."

"Henry, where are you?" Sue asked impatiently. "If you don't give us a sign, we're turning back."

"What was that?" Ellen noticed a dark figure in the distance in the field of tall grass where the swamp was dry. It appeared and disappeared.

"I don't see anything," Tanya remarked.

In a moment, the figure reappeared. It was humanoid but misshapen and as dark as night. With a lumpy head and red eyes, it seemed to glower at them. Its back slouched, and its long arms reached the ground where two short legs and long feet stood wide apart.

"Is th-that Henry Hamilton?" Tanya whispered.

"I think so," Ellen guessed. "Are we sure he's not luring us into a trap?"

"Why would he do that?" Sue wanted to know. "What would he gain from that?"

"He's evil," Ellen reminded her. "And messing with us is a form of entertainment to him."

"You're scaring me," Tanya accused.

"Lucy did say he was evil," Ellen recalled.

"Wouldn't he have killed us before now?" Sue argued.

The monster in the distance disappeared.

"Maybe he tried on the Sky Ride," Ellen theorized. "Maybe he's tried countless times before, and we just don't know about them."

"Ellen, stop," Tanya insisted. "Let's decide right now. Are we trusting him or not? Because, if we're not, we need to leave before it gets any darker."

"He said he'd help us if we helped him," Sue pointed out. "If we cooperate, we could save all those ghosts trapped at Peyton Randolph House."

Ellen sighed. "That's true."

"Guys, what are we going to do?" Tanya wanted to know.

The monster reappeared further in the distance.

Ellen scooped up her dog. "Let's follow him."

She led the way off the bridge into the high grass. Sue took out her flashlight to help guide them toward the thing in the distance. As they came within a few yards of it, it disappeared and reappeared further away.

They kept going through the high grass.

"There he is again." Ellen pointed.

They continued toward him just as he vanished again.

"He wasn't exaggerating when he said he was twisted and monstrous," Tanya muttered.

"Let's not antagonize what might be an evil demon," Sue warned.

"I don't see how calling him that is any better," Tanya argued.

Ellen sighed. "Can we not fight right now? Why hasn't he appeared again?"

Sue put her hand on her hips. "Maybe this is the spot."

Her flashlight flickered.

"Did he do that?" Tanya wondered.

"Henry," Ellen began, "if you made the flashlight flicker, can you do it again?"

The light flickered.

"Is the mass grave here, where we're standing?" Sue asked.

The light flickered.

"Let's put something here to mark the spot and get out of here," Tanya suggested. "We can call Bob later."

Ellen pointed. "What about those logs over there?"

"I'll hold the light for you," Sue offered.

Tanya rolled her eyes as she crossed the field. Ellen handed Moseby to Sue. Then, she and Tanya each dragged logs to where they were standing.

"I'm worried this isn't enough," Sue said. "Why don't one of you get that branch and use a rock to hammer it into the ground. We'll be able to see that better from a distance. I'd do it, but I think Moseby likes me best."

Ellen laughed as she and Tanya got to work. As she searched for a big rock, she said, "It's funny how the smallest people become the biggest bosses."

"She is pretty bossy," Tanya agreed.

"I'm just happy you called me small," Sue said with a grin. "But it's just occurred to me that we can pin this exact location on Google Maps, so no need to hammer anything after all."

"Good thinking, Sue," Ellen said, dropping the heavy rock she'd found. "I'm glad you know how to do that."

Sue handed Moseby over to Ellen so she could enter the pin on her phone. While they were standing there, Ellen felt like multiple eyes were watching them. She turned to see several transparent apparitions standing on the other side of the crossed logs from them.

"We-we found you," Ellen said in a friendly but frightened tone. "You can move on. Cross over to the other side. Your family is waiting for you."

The ghosts drifted toward them over the logs. Their faces were angry, demented even.

"Let's get out of here!" Tanya cried, before running toward the bridge.

Ellen followed Tanya, crying, "Come on, Sue!"

"Don't leave me, Ellen!" Sue, already panting, shouted.

Ellen turned to see her friend struggling through the high grass with the ghosts right on her heels.

"You aren't allowed to follow us!" Ellen shouted. "We mean to help you, but you have to wait!"

The apparitions did not heed her words but continued to follow Sue. Thank goodness the ghosts moved more slowly than her friend did. Ellen grabbed Sue by the arm and pulled her.

"Thanks for not leaving me behind," Sue said, panting.

"Don't talk. Run."

Moseby, who was in the crook of Ellen's other arm, whimpered. Ellen felt as if she were dragging Sue.

"Don't," Sue said, after they'd been running for at least a minute. "I'm going to fall if you keep pulling me like that. My legs can't keep up."

Ellen turned to see the apparitions had stopped a few yards away.

Relief surged through her. "They must be anchored to that spot. They aren't following us anymore."

She and Sue made their way to the bridge, where Tanya was waiting.

"Thanks a lot," Sue chastised Tanya.

"I wasn't thinking. I just reacted. I'm so sorry." Tanya was bawling her eyes out and shaking like a leaf in the wind.

"It's okay," Sue said. "I would have done the same thing if I were the skinny one."

"I was praying with all my might," Tanya said through her tears. "I shouldn't have left you."

"Everyone's okay, and that's what matters," Ellen insisted.

Ellen put Moseby down to let him walk. The canopy of leaves soon blocked the moonlight, making it impossible to see outside of their circles of light.

"What was that?" Tanya said after they were a few seconds into the woods.

"What?" Sue asked.

"I heard a stick snap, like they're still following us."

"It's probably just a deer," Ellen assured her, though she wasn't feeling as confident as she had sounded.

Ellen noticed that their pace away from the swamp was a lot faster than their pace toward it had been.

"Someone's following us," Tanya said again. "I can feel it."

"Maybe it's the creeper," Sue said. "Let's just get to the car."

When they finally reached the vehicle, they couldn't climb in fast enough.

Ellen sighed with relief once the car was heading toward Colonial Williamsburg.

"I wonder why those ghosts were so menacing toward us," Tanya said from the passenger's seat. "The ghosts at the house on Kestrel Court have been friendly, for the most part. I mean, one of them did try to drown Dave."

"Dave probably deserved it," Sue said from behind the wheel.

"True," Tanya admitted.

"Maybe it's because the spirits in the swamp haven't been around people," Ellen speculated. "Not like those on Kestrel Court have over the years."

"The ghosts at Peyton Randolph House have been around people," Sue argued. "And they're mean, too—not Eve, but some of the others."

"Good point," Ellen conceded. "Though the ghosts on Kestrel Court were part of the same community, and those at Peyton Randolph House are from different time periods. Maybe it's the sense of community that's different."

"That could be it," Tanya agreed.

"Well, I think we deserve a treat," Sue said. "And we have some time to kill before we have to meet Mark Murphy."

"What did you have in mind?" Tanya wanted to know.

Sue turned out of the park. "I'm kind of craving that gourmet mac and cheese we had at the Blue Talon Bistro. What do y'all think about that?"

"I'm game," Tanya said.

Comfort food was exactly what Ellen needed. "Let's do it."

CHAPTER FIFTEEN

Mr. Murphy's Wine Cellar

Sue parked the rental at the Visitor's Center in Colonial Williamsburg, where they climbed out and walked with Moseby to Peyton Randolph House. Most of the street cressets were no longer burning, but the chilly night was bright beneath the nearly full moon and starlit sky.

Mark Murphy, still wearing his colonial attire, stood with his bike in front of the great house next to an old whiskey barrel.

"Good evening, ladies."

"Hey, Mark." Sue waved.

"We're out of luck," he reported. "Jacinda already locked up and went home. I would have called you, but I didn't have your numbers, so I waited here for you. Sorry to have wasted your time."

"Oh, that's okay," Tanya said. "I'm exhausted anyway."

"Yeah, it's no big deal," Ellen added.

"Nevertheless, I thought I'd make it up to you by opening one of my colonial bottles of wine."

Tanya flapped a hand in the air. "You don't have to do that."

"Speak for yourself," Sue said with mock reproach. "I want to hear about the colonial wine."

Mark grinned. "Well, in addition to being a bellhop, actor, historian, and ghost enthusiast, I'm also somewhat of a wine connoisseur, and I have a cellar full of rare and valuable wine, including a bottle of Madeira, a Portuguese wine bottled in 1728—George Washington's favorite after-dinner drink."

"That must be worth a fortune," Ellen commented. "You don't want to open that for us."

"In case you haven't noticed," Mark began, "I'm not one to care much about money. I inherited my family's fortune, but I live a humble life doing the things I love, and I collect wine I enjoy drinking. Come on, my house is just a block this way."

"You live here, in Colonial Williamsburg?" Tanya asked, as they followed him in the opposite direction from the Visitor's Center.

"It's one of the perks of the job," he said. "That is, most actors don't live on-site, but some do, and I'm one of them. I love everything about my life here. I feel very fortunate."

Ellen and her friends followed Mark down Queen's Street, past the now defunct Market Square Tavern, to a tiny colonial house with white siding, a brick chimney, and two dormers. The house was surrounded by a white picket fence.

"This way, ladies," he said after opening the white picket gate.

He parked his bike next to the house and opened the front door.

"After you," he said, waving them through.

"Is Moseby welcome, too?" Ellen asked.

Mark patted Moseby's head. "Of course, he is. Like I said before, I love dogs."

It was dark inside until Mark turned on a lamp just inside to the left. To the right were stairs leading to the second floor.

"May I take your coats?" he offered. "I can put them in here."

He opened a closet that was directly across from the front door. It was filled with colonial attire and barely had room for three coats.

"That's okay," Ellen said. "I'm still a little chilled."

"Same," Tanya said. "It's so cold out there."

"We Texans aren't used to it," Sue added.

"Come on in and I'll get a fire going."

He led them into a small sitting area with a couch and one chair, where he turned on two more lamps. The three friends squeezed together on the couch. Ellen held Mo in her lap. Mark had kindling going in the fireplace in no time.

Then he stood up and clapped his hands. "Now, the wine. Excuse me. I'll be right back."

He walked past a small eating area and into a kitchen.

"This is such a charming house," Sue called out to him.

"Thank you. Would you like a tour? I'd be happy to show you. Everything is built exactly as it would have been in 1768, when it was originally built. I have a bedroom and full bath upstairs and a basement with a wine cellar downstairs."

"I'd love to see it," Tanya said as he returned with three glasses of wine.

"My pleasure," he said. "Let me just run upstairs and tidy up."

"You don't have to do that," Ellen said. "We don't need a tour."

"I insist."

Before anyone could reply, the young man had darted up the stairs and out of sight.

"This wine *is* delicious," Sue said.

Ellen thought so, too. "He didn't have to go to all this trouble."

"I know," Tanya agreed. "I feel bad. This must be so expensive."

Sue, who sat in the middle, lifted her glass. "Cheers, ladies."

They clinked glasses.

"Cheers," Ellen and Tanya echoed before drinking more of the delicious wine.

Mark returned downstairs. "Before we go up, I wonder if you would like to hear a song from a show we perform in front of the Governor's Palace. I'd love to know your opinion."

Ellen wasn't sure how to reply.

"We'd love it," Sue said, beaming.

Ellen jumped when the handsome Mr. Murphy broke out in a lovely but very loud alto singing voice from where he stood between them and the fireplace. She sipped the delicious wine and tried not to giggle as he finished his song about a homesick revolutionary war soldier.

The fire had begun to take, making the small room warm and cozy. Ellen felt sleepy now as Mr. Murphy's voice struck soothing low chords—so sleepy, she thought she might lay her head back and close her eyes for just a moment.

She startled awake when Mark Murphy said, "What did you think?"

"Lovely," Sue said sleepily. "Thank you for that."

"Yes," Ellen managed to say with heavy lids. "Very nice. Thank you."

"Are you ready for your tour now?" he asked.

"I might be too tired to make the stairs," Sue said with a yawn. "Y'all go on without me."

"Maybe we should head back," Tanya suggested. "I didn't realize how tired I was until we sat down."

"But I just cleaned up for you. Come on, ladies. I want you to see the house. I'm so proud of it and so grateful to live here."

"Okay," Ellen relented. "Lead the way. Come on, y'all. He's gone to all this trouble."

Ellen led Mo on his leash up the stairs after Mark, where the enthusiastic bellhop, actor, historian, ghost enthusiast, and wine connoisseur showed them his bedroom and full bath, complete with a colonial-sized tub. He told them about sixteenth-century architecture, but to sleepy Ellen, it sounded like blah, blah, and blah. Then they followed him back downstairs into the basement, and through a smaller door into his wine cellar, where it was very dark and cold.

"Pardon me a moment, ladies," he said somewhere near the door.

Ellen was waiting for him to turn on a light. Instead, she heard the slamming of the door.

"Mark?" Sue asked.

Through the door he said, "Please accept my apologies. I fibbed a bit. I *am* a wine connoisseur, but that wasn't a bottle of 1728 Madeira, it was a 1950 Merlot—still quite expensive. Also, I did not inherit my family's fortune. I come from a humble background. However, what I said about loving my life here is true, which is why I cannot allow you to ruin what I have worked for ten years to create."

"Mark?" Ellen, who felt numb and dazed, shouted. "What are you doing? Let us out of here!"

Sue's phone illuminated her face. "I'm calling 9-1-1."

"Is this really happening?" Tanya mumbled. "I feel like I'm dreaming. I'm so sleepy."

"Mark?" Ellen cried, fumbling toward the door.

"There's no service," Sue groaned.

Ellen searched for her phone in her purse. She could barely stay standing because she was so, so tired. She found her flashlight app and made her way to the door. It wouldn't budge. "Mark, please don't do this!"

"Can y'all try calling 9-1-1?" Sue urged in a panicky voice.

Ellen tried, but she, too, had no service.

"I need to sit down," Tanya said through her yawn. "I can't stay awake."

Ellen leaned back against the wall and scooched down to her bottom. Mo was whimpering beside her. She stroked his fur and closed her eyes. "Moseby-Mo, it's okay."

"He must have drugged us," Sue said sleepily. "What are we going to do?"

Ellen was too sleepy to answer. She leaned her head against the cold wall and relinquished all conscious thought.

"Ellen, save your phone battery," Sue said beside her.

Ellen's phone was taken from her hand, but she didn't care. She was too sleepy.

Moseby licked Ellen's face.

"It's okay," she said without opening her eyes.

She was just so sleepy.

Moseby let out his I-need-to-pee bark.

"I *do* have my pistol," Sue said. "I have it right here in my purse."

Ellen opened her eyes and blinked. It was pitch dark. "What's happening?"

"Oh, good," Tanya said, shining her phone light on Ellen before turning it toward the ceiling. "You're awake. Are you okay?"

Ellen rubbed her neck. "How long have we been down here?"

"Seven hours," Sue replied. "It's five-thirty in the morning."

Ellen glanced at Mo, who was telling her to take him outside. "I'm sorry, but I don't think he can hold it."

"I couldn't either," Tanya admitted. "There's a bucket over in that corner."

"Moseby doesn't know how to go in a bucket. Where's my phone?"

Sue handed Ellen her phone.

"Thanks." Ellen shined her phone light around the room. The room was maybe ten feet by ten feet with a concrete floor and brick walls. There was a bucket in one corner. Otherwise, the cold cellar was empty. "This place reminds me of Henry Hamilton's cell."

"You think he means to let us starve to death?" Sue wondered. "He can't let us go after this."

"He means to kill us, that's for sure," Ellen said. "But how, I don't know."

"Over a stupid curse," Tanya groaned. "I told y'all something was off about him. He's not all there."

"We need a plan," Sue said. "I was just telling Tanya about my gun. We've got to find a way to get him to come back down here, to come inside, so I can use it."

"What would make him come inside?" Ellen said angrily. "If he wants us dead, there's no reason to come in here. He wouldn't bring food or water or medicine." Tears formed in Ellen's eyes. "Why, Sue? Why would he come in here?"

"Tanya had an idea."

Moseby was peeing along the wall near the back of the room.

Ellen returned to her place on the floor beside Sue. "Let's hear it."

Tanya, who sat against the wall opposite them, leaned forward and shined her light toward the ceiling, casting a dim light throughout the room. "Well, first, we make enough noise to get him to come down here. Then we beg him not to let Moseby die, too."

"He said he's a huge fan of dogs," Sue reminded her. "It might just work."

Ellen's heart sank. "You want to use Mo as bait?"

"Do you have a better idea?" Sue challenged.

Ellen sighed. "No. But let me think. I just woke up."

"Regardless of what we decide about Mo," Sue began, "We should start making noise as soon as the sun comes up. I think that's around six or six-thirty."

"Someone will hear us, don't you think?" Tanya asked Ellen. "If we scream loud enough?"

Ellen was thinking about how much she wanted to see her children, grandchildren, and husband again. She was thinking about all the things she still wanted to experience with them. Yes, she'd had a good life. Yes, she was grateful. And yes, she was ready to accept God's will—but she hoped and prayed that she and her friends and Moseby would make it out of this alive.

She took a deep breath and sighed. "All we can do is try."

CHAPTER SIXTEEN

Jacinda Bloom

Ellen's throat felt like it was bleeding from screaming so much. Tired, thirsty, hungry, and sore, she squatted over the bucket and, for the first time since her captivity, was finally able to empty her bladder.

After she had finished, she used her phone light to find her way back to her spot between Moseby and Sue. Once settled, she checked the time. It was eleven at night.

"He should be home by now," she said as she turned off her phone to conserve the battery.

"If we can't hear him, he probably can't hear us," Sue surmised.

"No one can," Tanya groaned with despair.

They had each had three pieces of chocolate from Sue's purse, but that was the extent of their diet. The chocolate had only made them thirstier.

"If we make it out of here alive," Sue began, "I really am going to lose this weight. I know I say that all the time, but this isn't how I want to be remembered."

"Don't say that," Tanya pleaded. "Your weight is not how people will remember you. It doesn't define you."

"I'm always worried about my weight, too," Ellen admitted. "But the truth is, Tanya's right. We are so much more than the number on the scale. You won't be remembered for your weight. You'll be remembered for your wit, your humor, your intelligence, your bravery, your kind heart, and your compassion."

"Oh, Ellen," Sue said dismissively.

"I'm serious," Ellen insisted.

Tanya said, "Sue, don't you realize that you light up every room you enter? You're a people magnet. Everyone loves you. You make people feel comfortable. You make them laugh. You're so entertaining. People who know you don't think of your size when they think of you. They think of your amazing personality."

"Hear, hear," Ellen said.

"Y'all are making me cry," Sue chastised.

Just then, Ellen heard footsteps outside the door.

"He's coming!" Tanya whispered. "Get ready, Sue!"

Ellen turned on her phone and clicked on the light to see Sue turning off the safety on her pistol and pointing it at the door with a shaky hand.

"Don't hesitate," Ellen whispered. "Our lives are in your hands."

"If he opens that door," Sue whispered back, "I'm pulling the trigger."

Ellen hoped and prayed he would open it.

A knob rattled, a hinge creaked, and light penetrated the room. A shot went off. Tanya screamed as someone else hollered, "Police! Hold your fire!"

"Oh, my gawd!" Sue cried. "Did I kill anyone?"

Multiple flashlights scanned the room. Moseby started barking his ferocious "danger" bark.

Ellen found him and snatched him up, putting him in his cloth pooch carrier, as an officer shouted, "Everyone okay in here? Is anyone hurt?"

"We're okay," Tanya replied. "Oh, thank heavens! How did you find us?"

"Come on out, so we can get your statements," the officer said.

Another shouted, "Arrest Murphy and take him in!"

"Does that mean I didn't kill anyone?" Sue asked.

"No, ma'am. We're fine. Come on out."

"I might need help getting up," Sue said.

Spectators had gathered outside the small colonial home to gawk at the scene of the police officers escorting Ellen, Sue, Tanya, and Moseby into an ambulance parked nearby, where another officer took their statements and gave them something to eat and drink. They'd already spoken to one officer indoors. Across the yard, Ellen saw Mark Murphy in handcuffs being escorted to a police vehicle. She stared at him, willing him to look her way, but he didn't. When Ellen asked how the officers knew where to look for them—or knew that they were even missing—they said they'd received an anonymous tip. It wasn't until they were being dropped off by a police car an hour later at the parking lot of the Visitor's Center and approaching their rental car that they got their answer.

Waiting for them near their vehicle was Jacinda Bloom. She was still wearing her colonial attire—the clothing of a servant.

As the police car drove away, she said, "I know you ladies are exhausted, but I thought you might want to know who's responsible for rescuing you."

"Oh, Jacinda! Thank you!" Tanya cried.

"How did you know?" Sue asked.

"It's a bit of a story. Would you rather meet for breakfast in the morning to hear it? Or do you want to hear it now?"

"You decide," Ellen said. "It's nearly one in the morning. Maybe you need to get home."

"My next shift isn't until tomorrow at two, so I don't mind either way."

"I'd like to hear it now," Sue admitted, "if you don't mind. Where's your car?"

"I live nearby, so I walked."

"How did you know where to find our car?" Ellen wondered.

"I overheard you speaking with the police."

"Why don't you climb in and tell us your story while I drive you home?" Sue offered.

Once they were in the vehicle and pulling out of the Visitor's Center, Tanya, who sat in the back seat with Ellen and Moseby, asked, "Can we pick up food? I'm starving."

"Are you hungry, Jacinda?" Sue asked from behind the wheel.

"You aren't going to find anything open at this hour, unfortunately," she replied. "I have bread and lunchmeat at my house though, if you want sandwiches."

"That's okay," Ellen said. "We have snacks at home."

"Take a right here," Jacinda instructed.

"So, what happened?" Sue prompted.

"Okay. Tonight, Mark had another ghost tour. As per usual, he brought them to Peyton Randolph House, where I gave my tour—the same one you had, right?"

"Right," Sue said.

"We took them up to the oak-paneled room, like we always do, asking for a sign from Eve or any other spirit willing to communicate with us. The flashlights went on and off, like always."

"That isn't a trick, right?" Ellen asked.

"It's not a trick," Jacinda confirmed. "Oh, make another right up here . . . Anyway, tonight, as I was leaving the oak-paneled room—I'm always the last one to leave because part of my job is to secure the house for the night—anyway, as I was leaving the room, Eve—I think it was Eve—whispered in my ear."

Tanya leaned forward in the back seat. "What did she say?"

"She said, 'Mark has captives in his cellar.'"

"How did she know?" Ellen wondered.

"At first, I thought I had imagined it. Her voice was barely audible, right?"

"Right," Sue said. "Did she say anything else?"

"No . . . oh, turn left, turn left!"

Sue slammed on the brakes and then turned left.

Ellen was grateful that she'd been holding Mo, or he would have flown through the windshield.

"Sorry about that," Jacinda said. "My house is right there on the corner."

Sue pulled up to a tiny colonial house that resembled the one Mark lived in.

"So, then what happened?" Ellen asked once they were parked.

"I had just gone downstairs and was about to lock up when she appeared to me."

"Who? Eve?" Tanya asked.

"I think so. She looked the same as the apparition that spoke to you, Ellen."

"Did she say anything?" Ellen asked.

"She said, 'Call the police,'" Jacinda replied. "Then she disappeared, and I wet my britches. Oh, I can't believe I just said that."

"It's nothing we haven't done ourselves," Sue assured her. "Tanya does it almost every day."

"I do not!" Tanya denied.

"Well, not *every* day," Sue teased with a laugh.

"Anyway," Jacinda continued. "I knew I hadn't imagined *that*, so I called the police and told them that I wanted to remain anonymous but that I was ninety-nine percent sure that Mark Murphy had prisoners in his cellar. I gave them the address—he just lives a block away from me. They asked me a bunch of questions, and I said to please just check, and if I was wrong, they could arrest me. That's when I gave them my name and agreed to meet them in front of Mark's house."

"We can't thank you enough," Sue said again.

"You risked so much," Ellen pointed out. "Thank you for your kindness."

"Anyone would have done the same," Jacinda assured her.

"I wonder how Eve knew?" Tanya said again.

"I just couldn't believe it," Jacinda insisted. "Even when I told the police they could arrest me if I was wrong, I could barely believe it. Mark has always been such a nice guy. I considered him a friend."

"I guess you don't always know who the real monsters are," Ellen thought aloud.

"I guess not," Jacinda agreed. "Well, thank you for the ride."

"Wait, Jacinda." Sue leaned toward the passenger seat. "Can we treat you to breakfast or lunch tomorrow? We'd love the chance to thank you for all you did for us."

"That's not necessary, but thank you."

"That's a great idea," Tanya chimed in.

"Yes," Ellen agreed. "Please let us! We'd love to visit with you some more."

"In fact," Sue began, "we forgot to tell you that we may have found a way to break the curse on Peyton Randolph House."

"Really?" Jacinda asked with wide eyes. "That would be amazing."

"What time should we pick you up?" Sue asked.

"Let's do an early lunch," Jacinda suggested. "Pick me up at eleven?"

"Sounds perfect!" Sue said.

"See you then!" Ellen cried. "Good night!"

"Good night," the rest echoed.

Sue waited until Jacinda was safely inside before driving away.

"God, I'm glad to be alive," Tanya said a few minutes later.

Ellen started giggling. Soon all three of them were laughing out loud. Moseby glanced from Tanya to Ellen with a look of confusion, which only added to their laughter.

CHAPTER SEVENTEEN

Jolly Pond

The drive to Jolly Pond from Kestrel Court was only a ten-minute ride when Ellen and her friends and Moseby took the rental the following evening to meet the ghost of Henry Hamilton. Ellen felt the same apprehension she'd felt two nights before at Freedom Park. What did they really know about Henry Hamilton and his plans for them?

There was also the fact that he'd asked them to meet him the previous night, and they hadn't shown up. It wasn't their fault that they hadn't been able to keep their promise, but he didn't know that. Would he keep his end of their deal by helping to break the curse on the Peyton Randolph House? Or would he, instead, punish them for not showing up yesterday?

Before their lunch with Jacinda Bloom earlier that day, they'd called Vernon Blake, the shaman who had been recommended by Mary Pullen. They'd apologized for missing their appointment with him, explaining what had happened, and then had arranged for him to meet and have dinner with them at the house on Kestrel Court at seven that evening, after which they would attempt to connect with the ghost of Henry Hamilton. Vernon Blake wanted to speak to the ghost himself to assess whether Henry's intentions about lifting the curse were genuine.

They'd also phoned Bob Brooks to let him know about the possibility of additional bodies. Interestingly, his attitude about two mass graves was quite different than it had been when they had called to tell him about Sam Dickenson. Although Bob had initially planned to wait until January to visit Williamsburg, the promise of two mass graves containing the victims of lost American revolutionaries who'd been scalped under the orders of Lieutenant-General Henry Hamilton was too irresistible to put off. Bob decided to bring three members of his team to meet Ellen and her friends at the end of the week.

Ellen, Tanya, and Sue had revealed their plans for lifting the curse to Jacinda during their lunch date and had solicited her help in getting access to the house. Jacinda had assured them that she would be there every night at ten o'clock after her final tour. They were welcome to bring their medicine man any day of the week at that time.

"This is it," Tanya said from the passenger's seat, bringing Ellen from her reverie. "The southernmost point, according to Google Maps."

Sue slowed the vehicle and pulled off to the side of the road. Bundled in their coats and gloves, the three friends and dog made their way from the road through the dark woods toward the pond in the cold, windy night. At the water's edge, the pond stretched for hundreds of yards, glittering beneath the moon and stars. The water was still and shimmering, like a sheet of glass. It seemed almost mystical to Ellen as she stood there beside Mo, who sniffed at the pond with curiosity.

"We're late," Tanya complained. "We should have left fifteen or twenty minutes earlier."

"The days keep getting shorter and shorter," Sue reminded her. "I thought we had more time."

Ellen glanced around the pond and the surrounding line of trees. "I hope he shows. I hope he knows that it wasn't our fault that we couldn't be here last night."

"I don't know if I want to see him again, to be honest," Tanya admitted. "We think he's showing us the location of mass graves, but why do we trust him? Lucy said he's evil. Eve said he's evil. His own journal admitted that he's evil."

"We *don't* trust him," Sue replied. "But we need his help, remember? We can't break the curse at Peyton Randolph House without him."

"That's the only reason I'm here," Tanya agreed. "Let's just hope he's not deceiving us."

Ellen shuddered. The night seemed colder. Worried about Mo, she scooped him up and put him into his cloth pooch carrier to keep them both warm.

"Over there," Sue said, pointing.

It was so dark that Ellen could barely make out the misshapen figure of Henry Hamilton where he appeared near the shore of the pond and disappeared almost as quickly. If it hadn't been for his bright, red eyes, Ellen might not have seen him at all.

"Is that a boat?" Tanya pointed to what appeared to be a small, aluminum boat lying in the tall grass near the pond where the apparition had been.

"Please tell me he doesn't want us to get inside that boat," Sue groaned.

Sue's flashlight flickered.

The three friends jumped with surprise. Ellen's heart began to race.

"Henry, was that you that made Sue's light flicker?" Ellen asked. "If so, please do it again."

Sue's light flickered again.

"If you don't want us to get in the boat, make my light flicker," Sue commanded.

The light remained constant for nearly a minute before Sue groaned again.

"We don't all have to get in the boat," Ellen assured her. "We'll need someone to push us off."

Tanya frowned. "Only one needs to go, right?"

Ellen blanched. "You want me to go alone?"

"Not if you don't want to," Tanya promised.

"Why would I want to?"

"I'll hold onto Mo for you," Sue offered.

Ellen handed Moseby over to her friend, and then the three trudged through the tall grass toward the aluminum boat. When they reached it, they found a paddle lying in the bottom, but there were no life jackets or floating boat cushions, only a bench across the middle and another at the back of the boat.

"Henry?" Ellen began. "Are you sure this boat won't sink?"

Their lights remained constant.

"He isn't sure," Tanya said nervously. "Are we sure we want to do this?"

Tanya's light flickered.

"*You're* sure, Henry," Ellen conceded, "but *we* aren't."

Suddenly, Moseby began to screech.

"Mo?" Sue looked him over.

Ellen ran to her side, feeling like her heart was clenched in a tight ball. "Moseby, what's wrong?" She'd never heard him make a sound like that before.

He was trembling and screeching a high-pitched wail.

"It's Henry!" Tanya guessed. "Henry, stop! We'll go in the boat!"

Immediately, Moseby's screeching stopped, and he stopped trembling. He licked Ellen's nose and curled against Sue.

If Ellen hadn't already despised Henry Hamilton, she sure as hell did now. Full of contempt, she marched to the boat, where Tanya was already sitting on the back bench. Ellen shoved the boat to the edge of the bank and jumped in, nearly toppling over.

"Ellen!" Tanya cried. "Sit down!"

Clinging to the sides of the boat which were only three feet apart, Ellen sat on the bench, fuming and too angry to care whether she fell over. "What now, asshole?"

"Ellen!" Tanya warned. "I wouldn't taunt him if I were you."

Tanya took up the paddle as Sue pushed the front of the boat away from the bank with her foot.

"Take care of Mo!" Ellen shouted to Sue. "Is he okay?"

"He's fine," Sue promised. "I'll take care of him." Then she added, pointing, "Look over there."

Ellen turned to see the misshapen form of Henry Hamilton. Tanya struggled with the paddle.

"Give it to me," Ellen insisted.

Tanya was thin and in great cardiovascular shape, but Ellen had her beat in brute strength. She pushed the paddle through the water toward the apparition. It disappeared and reappeared a few yards further out. She continued to paddle, cursing Henry Hamilton in her head.

The ghost disappeared as Ellen reached him. He appeared again a few yards in the distance. Ellen paddled toward him as he disappeared again.

When she reached the spot where he had last appeared, Ellen glanced around, but the monster did not reappear.

"I don't see him," Tanya said.

"Is this the spot?"

Tanya's flashlight flickered.

Ellen sighed with relief, tired from paddling. Plus, it was colder on the water. She couldn't wait to be back at the house on Kestrel Court in front of a cozy fire. "Can you pin this location to your Google Maps?"

"I don't know how."

Ellen didn't either. She turned back to find Sue and the bank too far away for conveying instructions.

"Hold on," Tanya said, tapping her phone. "I found a tutorial on YouTube."

While Tanya watched her video, Ellen noticed the water, which had been as calm and still as a sheet of glass, begin to stir around their boat.

"I don't like the look of this," Ellen murmured.

The water churned and chopped, rocking them. Then a pair of transparent hands with long, bony fingers reached out of the water and grabbed the side of the boat.

"Tanya?" Ellen said through trembling lips. "Do you see what I see?"

"Oh my God. Hit them with the paddle."

"What good will that do? It's a ghost! Just hurry and pin, will you, please?"

Another pair of hands reached out and grabbed the other side of the boat.

"We come in peace!" Ellen announced. "We're here to help you to move on, to find your eternal rest. Look for the light. I pray that God's heavenly angels—"

Ellen was cut short when the boat began to rock even harder, threatening to toss them overboard.

"Tanya! Hurry the heck up!"

"I've almost got it. Hang on." Tanya moved from the bench to the bottom of the boat, so she could use both hands to pin the location.

"Whoa!" Ellen cried when the boat leaned sharply to the right. "Please don't hurt us! We came to find you, to help you find peace. Please!"

"Got it!" Tanya cried. "Paddle!"

Ellen thrust the end of the paddle in the churning water and pushed with all her might. The ghost hands held for a few more moments and then disappeared beneath the surface. The water, too, stopped churning. Ellen didn't slow down, however. She kept going at full speed until they had reached the shore.

"Pull us up onto the bank," she said to Sue.

"Get a little closer first. I don't want to get wet."

Ellen used the paddle to push them as far up on the bank as she could manage—which wasn't very far at all. But it was enough for Sue to grab ahold with both her hands and pull. She pulled so hard that she fell in the grass on her backside, yelping as she landed.

Ellen jumped from the front of the boat to Sue's side. "Are you alright?"

"I'm okay. Just help me up. I'm sure I bruised my hip, but nothing's broken."

Ellen took Mo's leash from Sue and then pulled Sue to her feet just as Tanya hopped from the boat.

"Are you hurt?" Tanya asked.

"Probably bruised but nothing's broken," Sue repeated. "What about y'all? I thought I heard you screaming."

Ellen scooped up Mo. "Let's get back to the car, and we'll tell you all about it."

CHAPTER EIGHTEEN

The Spiritualist

On the way home from Jolly Pond, Ellen and her friends picked up "Hot Holly" subs from the College Delly and gourmet mac and cheese from the Blue Talon Bistro, so they would have food to feed themselves and their seven-o'clock guest.

Vernon Blake arrived five minutes early, but Ellen and her friends were ready when he rang at the door. Short and round and not much taller than Sue, he reminded Ellen of a Native American version of Santa Claus—though Vernon's beard was styled in a long and narrow—and more eastern—fashion.

His smile and his laugh, more than the white beard, gave off the Santa vibe. "Happy Holidays. I hope you like brownies." He handed over a paper plate wrapped in foil.

"Thank you, Mr. Blake," Sue said. "We love brownies."

"You didn't need to bring anything," Tanya insisted.

"But we're glad you did," Ellen said with a smile.

Moseby ran between the man's legs and then put his paws on Mr. Blake's shins, asking for attention.

The visitor patted Moseby's head. "Hello there, buddy."

"That's Moseby," Ellen explained. "Come on in and have a seat."

Although Sue's dining room table had been delivered, they sat around the glass table in the breakfast nook, where they had already laid out the food.

Their guest asked if he could lead them in a prayer. They bowed their heads while he thanked the creator for the blessings of good food and good company.

"Thank you for that, Mr. Blake," Sue said. "Would you like a glass of wine with your meal?"

"Oh, please call me Vernon. And no thanks. I don't drink."

"Cup of hot tea?" Tanya offered.

"That sounds nice. Thank you."

Tanya poured the tea and set the cream and sugar in the middle of their table.

Vernon hadn't yet taken a sip or a bite when he said, "I'm very intrigued by your proposition. What have you managed to glean from this presence which you believe is the ghost of Henry Hamilton?"

"Well, we don't really know if we can trust him," Ellen admitted. Then she recounted what had happened to her dog.

"Multiple sources, including one written by Henry Hamilton himself, have described him as evil," Tanya added, before taking a bite of her sub.

Sue took a sip of her wine. "But we think he showed us the locations of two mass graves of American revolutionary families who were scalped by Indians under his orders."

"Three, if you count the cellar here," Tanya clarified.

"He's trying to make amends," Vernon concluded with a nod.

"That's how it seems," Ellen agreed. "Our anthropologist friend from the University of Oklahoma is coming with a team to investigate the other two mass graves. The remains found here have already been examined, and those findings have corroborated what the ghosts have told us." Then she added, "Almost all, that is." She told him the story of Sam Dickenson.

"Getting Bob to come was part of our deal with Henry," Sue explained. "We help Bob find the bones and bring peace to Henry's victims and, in exchange, Henry translates the medicine needed to break the Powhatan curse on Peyton Randolph House."

"Our friend Mary said you were the shaman to help us," Ellen chimed in before taking another bite of her sub.

"I prefer the term spiritualist . . . this food is delicious, by the way. Thank you for providing it."

"No, thank you for spending your Friday night with us," Sue replied before swallowing down more of her wine.

"It's my pleasure." He took another bite and, after a moment, stated, "There are some things I want you to understand before we get started. The spiritual beliefs of Native Americans differ from tribe to tribe—and even from person to person within a tribe. Many are Christians. Some have combined principles from Christianity with those from their ancestral beliefs. And yet others have created personal belief systems based on many different things. I am the latter. I do not represent the Pamunkey tribe."

"Pamunkey?" Ellen repeated. "You mean you aren't Powhatan?"

Vernon chuckled. "You should know that before the arrival of the English, my people lived here for over twelve thousand years. The Powhatan Indian lands included the tidewater Virginia area, from the south side of the James River all the way north to the Potomac River, and parts of the eastern shore, too. We started as six tribes totaling over thirty thousand people, and, by the time the English arrived, we were more than thirty tribes. I think you know how those numbers dwindled over time. The Pamunkey is just one tribe that can trace its heritage back to the Powhatan nation."

"I see." Ellen glanced at her friends before returning her gaze to Vernon. "But you think you can break the curse?"

"I can try. You see, blessings and curses are created with words. Curses are the opposite of blessings, and vice versa. Because they are created with words, they can only be broken with words in the same language in which they were made."

"Which is where Henry comes in," Sue interjected.

"And sometimes curses can be transferred to an object," Vernon explained. "In your case, it sounds as if the object is Peyton Randolph House itself. This means that we will need to put the curse into a different object and break it and flush it away, to be thorough."

"Do you have something in mind?" Tanya wondered.

"An egg works best."

Ellen never would have imagined that Vernon would suggest an egg, but she supposed there were still so many things about the supernatural that she did not know or understand.

She took another sip of her tea. "Why do you think this curse was put on the house in the first place? Do you believe in the theory that Pocahontas and her father are buried beneath it?"

Vernon finished chewing his food before saying, "It's possible. The Pamunkey have another site that is believed to be the final resting place of Wahunsenacawh, also known as Powhatan. And his daughter is believed to have passed in England. But, if he and his daughter *are* buried beneath the house, that would explain why a curse was made—but it would not have been made by the dead. It would have been made by the living. One thing most Native Americans have in common is the belief that the spirits of the dead, who act as guides for the living, dwell close to their place of burial. Therefore, when graves are disturbed, it is a traumatic blow to native peoples. The living, and not their ancestors, feel the anger required to enunciate a curse."

"That makes sense," Sue said, before taking another bite of mac and cheese. "But if you speak with your ancestors, can't you ask one of them to break the curse in the Powhatan language? Maybe using Henry as an interpreter is unnecessary."

"Unfortunately, I don't communicate with ancestors that far back. I don't know how to ask for their help."

"So, what do we do next?"

"Before we attempt to use the ghost that has been following you as an interpreter, I need to test his intentions, to be sure they are noble and pure. We don't want to put ourselves in danger or to find ourselves strengthening rather than breaking the ancient curse."

"True," Tanya agreed.

"How will you test his intentions?" Ellen asked.

"I'm going to allow him to possess me."

After they had finished their meal, Tanya made a pot of coffee while Ellen and Sue rinsed the plates and placed them in the dishwasher. While they worked in the kitchen, Vernon lit a sage smudge stick, blew out the flame, and let the smoke fill the air before setting it in Ellen's abalone bowl in the middle of the glass table of the nook. He washed the smoke over his body and moved in a kind of dance. As he did so, he shook a rattle and sang a song that sounded something like, "Nah, tama, key, win, we, wah. Nah, tama, key, win, we, wah."

Before getting started, Vernon had shown them his rattle and had explained that it was made from a dried gourd. The roundest part of the gourd had been carved open where a thin piece of leather had been stretched across and secured to it, like a small drum. Inside were rocks and beans that made one sound when they hit the gourd and another when they hit the leather. And the rocks made a different sound than the beans. He said the act of shaking the rattle and of adding his own voice to the sounds put different elements of the earth in conversation with one another. The skin of the animal held the animal spirit, the gourd and the beans held plant spirits, and the stones held mineral spirits. As he sang, he called upon those spirits to guide him in his journey to communicate with the dead.

Once he'd finished his song, he asked Ellen and her friends to turn off the lights and join him at the round table, where he'd lit their three pillar candles.

"Are you sure this is a good idea?" Ellen asked—not for the first time. "Inviting a known evil entity to possess you?"

"Trust me," Vernon replied. "I've done this before."

"What should we do while you're being possessed?" Sue wanted to know.

"You each have an important role in this. One of you must shake the rattle. Another one of you must sing the song. And the last one of you must be ready to ask questions of the spirit once he possesses me."

Tanya picked up the rattle. "Sue's got the best singing voice."

Sue shot Tanya a dirty look. Then, turning a nicer expression to Vernon, she said, "I don't know the words."

"In this case, the words are less important than the sound of your voice in conversation with the spirits. But try saying something simple, such as, 'Nah-tama-key-win.' That means *help*."

"That's a mouthful to say when you're in grave danger," Sue pointed out. "Maybe that's why so few of you survived."

"Sue!" Tanya chastised.

Ellen felt her cheeks go pale.

Vernon laughed. "You're a funny one, aren't you?"

"That's what I've been told—more times than I can count."

"But she can't count past ten." Ellen gave Sue another angry look while mouthing *What were you thinking?*

"He knows I was only kidding. Right, Vernon?"

"Of course." He chuckled again.

"Now, would you mind repeating that word for help?" Sue asked. "I'll write it down."

"Nah-tama-key-win."

Sue wrote out the syllables as best as she could on a notepad before looking up and giving them a nod. "Okay. I'm ready when you are."

"Wait," Ellen insisted. "Is there anything we should do if things get out of hand? What if Henry doesn't want to leave your body?"

"Blow out the candles. The spirit needs energy to possess me, so deprive him of it, and say words of banishment as you bathe me in sage. But I doubt it will come to that. Okay?"

Ellen gave him a reluctant nod. She hoped he knew what he was doing.

Tanya began shaking the rattle. Sue started singing.

"Maybe not quite so loudly," Vernon said to Sue.

Ellen and Tanya exchanged grins as Sue blushed and lowered her voice.

Vernon closed his eyes and opened them again, showing only the whites. "If I am an arsehole, Ellen, then you are a bloody twat."

Ellen straightened her back, her jaw hanging open.

Sue stopped singing. Tanya had to poke her to get her going again.

"Henry?" Ellen finally asked.

"Well, this isn't Kublai Khan, now, is it?"

Heat raced to Ellen's cheeks. "I only called you an asshole because of what you did to my dog."

"You are the most exasperating person I have ever met—dead or alive. I would prefer the company of Thomas Jefferson to yours. A picnic short of a sandwich—that's what you are. I did that to your dog, you dimwit, because I needed you to hurry out there on Jolly Pond. I do not have infinite amounts of energy to make myself appear to you. Your hesitation was going to cost us the mission."

"If you don't have infinite amounts of energy," she began, "then you'd better stop berating me and prove your good intentions to the kind spiritualist you're currently occupying before he refuses to work with you."

"Good point. But hear this. I have a message from your father—a very specific message. He gave it to me while your family was crossing over the other night."

Ellen leaned over the table, nearly upsetting the abalone bowl. "My father? What did he say?"

"I may never tell you. First, let's see how well you cooperate."

"You manipulative . . . I don't believe you."

"He mentioned your brother, Jody."

Ellen glanced at her friends who were having a hard time with their jobs because they were too distracted by Henry's words.

"What do you want me to do?" Ellen asked.

"You already know. I want those remains found and acknowledged. I want the souls, which have been trapped for over two centuries, freed at last. I have learned that heaven and hell are different for everyone. Heaven is peace and a sense of community with loved ones. Hell is loneliness, misery, and isolation. I am in hell, and the only way out is to atone for what I have done."

Ellen should have known that he was only motivated by self-interest.

"Fine," she said. "Now explain how you will help with the curse."

"Eve told me that all who die at Peyton Randolph Place are trapped there."

"Her son isn't trapped."

"No. He died elsewhere. Lucky bloke. Those who are trapped are bored. Many of them entertain themselves at the expense of the living, which explains why so many deaths have occurred there over the centuries. The curse itself isn't directly responsible for the deaths. It's an entrapment curse. But by lifting it, the souls can leave and no longer torment the living."

"And can you act as a Powhatan interpreter for Vernon Blake?" she asked.

"I do not know all the Powhatan words, but I know enough to provide a decent translation, I think."

"You think?" Ellen felt her heart begin to race. "You mean this might not work?"

"Nothing in life is a sure thing until it becomes a historical thing—and even then, it can be rubbish."

"Very well." Ellen frowned. "Our anthropologist friend arrives tomorrow. You have my word that we'll help the souls of your victims."

"Cheers then."

"Wait. Should we try to lift the curse at Peyton Randolph House tomorrow night?" Ellen asked.

"Not until the souls of my victims are free."

"That could take months. Why should those other spirits suffer another day? I thought death had changed you. Or do you still care about no one but yourself?"

"Fine!" he shouted through the body of Vernon. "Tomorrow night. But if you want to know your father's message, you will have to wait until all the souls at Colby Swamp and Jolly Pond are free."

Vernon's eyes closed, and his head slumped forward. He quickly recovered himself and said to Tanya and Sue, "You can stop now."

Tanya handed over the rattle. "Are you okay?"

"Never better." Vernon climbed to his feet. "Thank you for a pleasant evening, ladies. The food was brilliant. Shall we meet at Peyton Randolph House tomorrow at ten o'clock in the evening?"

Ellen climbed to her feet. "That would be great. But you don't have to rush off. Don't you want a brownie and some coffee?"

"As tempting as that sounds, I'm afraid I must decline." He headed for the door.

Ellen and her friends followed.

"Don't you want to talk about Henry Hamilton?" Sue asked. "Did you find his intentions pure?"

"Pure as honey. Honestly, I'm knackered. And besides, what more is there to say? I have what I need from the man. Let's hope he comes through for us tomorrow."

Moseby jumped up from where he'd been sleeping on the family room sofa and followed the group to the front door.

"Goodbye, then," Tanya said. "See you tomorrow."

"Ta-ta for now," the spiritualist said as he left through the door. They watched him walk to the curb, where his yellow Volkswagen Beetle was parked, and climb in.

Ellen closed the door and leaned against it. "You don't think . . . ah, never mind."

"You think he's still possessed?" Tanya wondered.

"That's exactly what I was thinking," Sue admitted.

Tanya covered her mouth. "What if he is? What should we do?"

"Whatever it takes," Ellen assured her.

"Should we follow him home?" Tanya wondered. "If Henry stays in there too long, won't it be harder to get him out?"

"I don't know that one day will make a difference," Sue speculated. "Besides, we don't really know for sure that he's in there."

Ellen crossed her arms. "After we use him to break the curse tomorrow night, we'll do whatever it takes to exorcise him the hell out of there."

"If he's even in there," Tanya added.

"Let's finish that bottle of wine," Sue suggested.

"Oh, and don't forget Vernon's brownies," Ellen reminded them.

As they returned to the breakfast nook, Tanya asked, "Ellen, do you really think Henry has a message from your father? Or is he just manipulating you?"

"How could he know about Jody?" Ellen pointed out. "I haven't spoken about my brother, have I?"

"No, not that I recall," Sue said. "Any idea what that message might be?"

Ellen took a deep breath as tears filled her eyes. "No, but I'm dying to know."

CHAPTER NINETEEN

The Curse

The next morning, Ellen and her friends spent a leisurely day around the house on Kestrel Court hanging wall art and adding other decorative touches while discussing strategies for exorcising Henry Hamilton from the body of Vernon Blake. They went over the instructions they'd received from their friend, Father Yamamoto, who had helped them with exorcisms in the past.

"We can use Vernon's rattle to purify the air," Tanya pointed out. "And his sage smudge stick for good measure."

"How will we bind him?" Ellen wondered as she held a painting over the sofa in the living room. "Here?"

"That will be the tricky part." Sue waved her palm through the air. "An inch to your left."

"I carry my holy water in a small spray bottle in my purse," Ellen informed them as Tanya marked the spot for the nail, "so, I've got that part covered."

"There's rope in the basement," Tanya recalled. "Sue can threaten him with her gun if he doesn't cooperate."

Sue frowned. "That won't work. Henry's already dead and knows we wouldn't hurt Vernon."

"True," Tanya conceded. "So, what are we going to do?"

"Let's take the rope and look for an opportunity to overtake him," Ellen suggested. "Three against one are good odds."

Later, in the afternoon, they met Bob Brooks and his team of three students at Freedom Park to show them the location of one of the mass graves. Bob used ground penetrating radar to confirm the presence of human remains. He told Ellen and her friends that he would begin the tedious process of securing a permit from the city to designate the area as an official archaeological site.

At Jolly Pond, Bob used underwater camera technology to explore the area Tanya had pinned on Google Maps. Ellen, Tanya, and Sue watched from the bank. Whereas the process at Freedom Park had taken less than forty-five minutes, the underwater exploration took several hours. Ellen and her friends left to have dinner before any conclusive evidence had been discovered.

At nine-thirty in the evening, after finally receiving confirmation from Bob that the mass grave at Jolly Pond had been found, Ellen and her friends filed into their rental car, leaving Moseby behind, and drove to the Colonial Williamsburg Visitor's Center, where they parked and then trekked in the cold night to Peyton Randolph House.

It was cold but lovely out, with twinkling stars and a waning gibbous moon in a clear sky, but Ellen worried that Henry was going to deceive them by not breaking the curse and by remaining in possession of Vernon Blake's body. They were all on edge about saving their new friend from their old adversary.

"What if he doesn't show up?" Tanya wondered as they approached the house from behind.

"Let's cross that bridge when we come to it," Sue insisted.

"And like you said," Ellen began, "we don't really know for sure that Henry is in there."

When they reached the front lawn of Peyton Randolph House, they found the spiritualist's yellow Volkswagen Beetle illegally parked on it with its front bumper bent and pressed against the old whiskey barrel.

"What on earth?" Sue cried.

"Is he in there?" Tanya wondered.

"No," Ellen said as they got closer. "He must be waiting inside the house."

They knocked and were welcomed inside by Jacinda Bloom, who was wearing her colonial attire.

"I'm not too sure about your shaman," she whispered to them in the entryway. "I think he's drunk."

"But he doesn't drink," Tanya replied. The wheels seemed to be slowly turning in her head when she nodded and added, "But Henry does."

"What are you talking about?" Jacinda wanted to know.

Since they were alone in the entryway, they told the tour guide their theory.

"That explains a lot," she said when they were finished. "Come upstairs. He's waiting in the second-floor parlor outside the oak-paneled bedroom."

They hadn't climbed but a few steps when Tanya missed one and fell. She rolled back and hit her head on the wooden floor in the entryway.

"Tanya?" Ellen rushed to her side and helped her up.

"My head." As she tried to walk, she limped and said, "I've also done something to my ankle."

"Can we move the ritual down here?" Sue asked Jacinda.

"Let's ask your shaman," Jacinda said. "He chose the spot."

Ellen followed Jacinda to the upstairs parlor, where they found Vernon—or Henry—snoring in the corner of a sofa wearing the same clothes he'd been wearing the previous evening—a brown leather jacket over a blue, button-down shirt untucked with a pair of blue jeans. Ellen cleared her throat, and the short, round man jumped to his feet.

"Pardon me, ladies." Then to Ellen, he added, "You're quite tidy, aren't you?"

"I don't know what you mean," she replied. "But we're ready to lift this curse, if you are."

"Yes, of course. Fine."

"Do you mind if we perform the ritual downstairs?" Jacinda asked.

"I thought you said this area had the most activity?" he objected.

"Yes, but Tanya's hurt and can't make the climb."

"Of course. Well then. After you."

Jacinda led the way downstairs. Henry wobbled and looked as though he could barely maintain his balance.

"Did you bring an egg?" Ellen asked, unable to keep the irritation from her voice.

"No, I did not bring an egg. Why would I?"

"You said it was important for breaking the curse," Sue reminded him as they reached the landing.

"Ah, yes. I did. Didn't I?" He wobbled into the first-floor parlor, where Tanya was already seated near the fireplace in a wingback chair. He fell onto another sofa. After landing on his seat, he shifted to pull his phone from his back jean pocket.

"I've got eggs at home," Jacinda offered. "Should I grab a few?"

"Funny little thing, isn't it?" Vernon commented as his fingers tapped around on the phone.

Ellen heard her phone buzz. She dug it out of her purse. There was a text was from Vernon. It read, *Don't let on you know, or he'll just dig in deeper. Carry on as planned but be careful. The curse doesn't want to be broken. I need coffee.*

Ellen raised her brows before showing the text to her friends.

Vernon's still in partial control, Sue texted in their group chat.

"Should I step out for the eggs?" Jacinda asked again.

"If you don't mind," Ellen replied. "And maybe some ice for Tanya's ankle? I'll drive you, and we can pick up coffee on the way back."

"Sounds good."

Sue tapped the shoulder of the spiritualist, who had begun to doze. "Hello . . . Vernon? Do you have your rattle and sage smudge stick?"

"Out in the car," he said sleepily.

His head fell back into the corner of the sofa, and he began to snore.

"I'll go get them and be back in a jiffy," Ellen remarked as she held out her hand for the key to the rental car.

Sue handed it over. "Be careful. Remember, the curse doesn't want to be broken."

"I promise," Ellen assured her.

Jacinda, who was ahead of her, opened the door and cried, "Oh, no! His car is being towed."

Jacinda rushed out to meet the tow truck driver. Ellen followed but was slow compared to the younger woman.

When Ellen caught up to her, the tow truck was already pulling away, and wouldn't stop no matter how frantically Ellen waved her arms in the air.

Jacinda handed over a card. "He wouldn't budge, but he gave me this. It's where they're taking it."

Ellen pulled out her phone and looked up the address on Google Maps. "It's only six minutes away. Want to come with me? We can swing by your place after."

"Do you really need the rattle and sage?" Jacinda wondered. "Can't we use something else?"

"I don't want to throw Vernon off," Ellen replied as she began walking toward the Visitor's Center behind Peyton Randolph House. "He's already fighting for control over his own mind and body."

"True."

As Ellen ascended the pathway, she lost her footing and landed on her knees.

"Ah!" she cried as she tried to get up. "This isn't icy, is it?"

"It's not cold enough to be. It's forty degrees. Are you okay?"

"Yeah. I think I may have skinned my knees and ruined these pants, though."

"Do you think it's true, what Sue said about the curse not wanting to be broken?" Jacinda asked as they reached the rental car. "Do you think that's why Tanya and now you have fallen tonight?"

"I don't know. They could be coincidences." Ellen climbed behind the wheel.

Jacinda got in the passenger's side. "Thank you for doing this—for trying to break the curse. I've always felt sorry for the ghosts trapped in that house—even the mean ones."

"It's what I do—my friends and I. We've dedicated the past six or seven years to it." Ellen started the engine.

"It must feel nice, to know you're doing something good in the world."

Ellen turned out of the parking lot, and taking her cue from her phone's navigation, turned left onto the main road. "It has filled us with a great sense of purpose. You're welcome to join us tomorrow night for the crossover ceremonies of those mass graves I told you about, if you're not working, that is."

"I don't work on Sundays."

"Perfect. Please come. I'll text you the details."

"What do you do at a crossover ceremony?"

"We light candles, sometimes sing songs, and we pray to God's heavenly angels to guide the lost souls to their everlasting peace."

"That sounds beautiful. Do you think my church choir could join, too?"

"That would be wonderful. Do you think they would?" Ellen looked down at her phone to see where to turn next.

"Watch out!" Jacinda cried suddenly.

Ellen looked up to see a big truck driving toward her in her lane. She pumped the breaks and swerved to the shoulder, just grazing the other vehicle.

She sat there, catching her breath. The truck didn't even stop to see if they were okay.

"That was close," Jacinda said with wide eyes. "I'm beginning to think we're in mortal danger."

"Do you want to turn back?"

"No. It's okay. It's not that far to go."

Once she'd recovered, Ellen eased back onto the main road toward the tow yard.

When they arrived, the driver of the tow truck had just finished parking the yellow Beetle in the asphalt lot, which was surrounded by a six-foot chain-link fence. The gate was padlocked.

Ellen pulled in front of the gate and hollered to the driver as he was about to climb back into his tow truck, "Excuse me! Sir?"

"We open at eight in the morning," he hollered back.

"Can I please just get something out of that vehicle? It's an emergency."

"Come back at eight in the morning." The man climbed behind the wheel and slammed the door shut before exiting through a back gate.

Ellen returned to her rental and drove around the outside of the lot, hoping to cut him off. By the time she reached the back gate, the driver was already locking it and was about to hop into his truck again.

She rolled down the windows of the rental. "Wait! Please!"

The man ignored her, returned to his tow truck, and drove through a ditch to avoid her vehicle.

"What is wrong with people?" Ellen cried with frustration. "Why couldn't he give us a few minutes of his time?"

"This probably happens to him all the time," Jacinda speculated. "I bet he isn't paid enough to stay later than he has to, especially on a Saturday night."

"But this is an emergency."

"I'm sure that's true for everyone."

Ellen sat there for a moment, thinking. If they waited to attempt to break the curse tomorrow, would they still have the cooperation of Henry Hamilton? He knew Ellen and her friends wanted the souls of his victims to find peace as much as he did. This left them with no leverage. None. Even worse, what if Henry chose to remain in possession of Vernon Blake rather than seek eternal rest? He was drunk and vulnerable now. Putting off the ritual until tomorrow meant risking everything. They might lose their chance of breaking the curse and exorcising Henry from Vernon.

Ellen drove the car around to the first gate, which was closer to the Beetle, and parked. "I'm climbing the fence."

"What? I should do it. I'm in better shape. No offense."

"I don't want you to ruin your costume. I'm sure it's expensive."

"But what if you hurt yourself?"

"I wouldn't be able to live with myself if I didn't try."

"Let me at least help you."

Together they approached the fence.

"You should climb over there, by that pickup," Jacinda suggested. "You can use the truck to help climb down. Then use it again to climb back over."

"Great idea."

"I'll give you a boost." Jacinda linked her fingers together for Ellen's foot.

Ellen hesitated. "I don't want to hurt you."

"I can handle it."

Ellen grabbed ahold of the fence, pushed off Jacinda's hands, and stuck the toe of her boot into the fence for a higher footing. Then she grabbed the top of the fence, swinging her other leg over. Fortunately, she could reach the top of the cab of the truck. She allowed herself to slide over and halfway fall onto her already hurt knee. When she landed, a car alarm scared her into action. She jumped into the bed of the truck, climbed over the tailgate, and ran to the yellow Beetle.

Fortunately, it wasn't locked, and she was able to grab the rattle and the smudge stick from the passenger's seat, but not before noticing empty wine bottles and chocolate wrappers on the floorboard. This made her realize that Vernon's life had been in jeopardy, as Henry had been drinking and driving.

With the alarm still ringing throughout the lot, she climbed back onto the bed of the pickup and then onto the hood of the cab.

"Almost there, Ellen!" Jacinda cheered from the other side of the fence.

"Catch the smudge stick, will you?" Ellen dropped it over.

"Got it. Now, hurry!"

Ellen held the rattle in her mouth as she swung her leg over and climbed down the fence. Then she and Jacinda raced to the rental car and drove away.

"You were amazing," Jacinda said from the passenger's seat.

"Thanks. It was all adrenaline. I'm sure I'll be feeling it soon."

"I have Ibuprofen at home, if you want some."

"Thank you. I should carry that stuff in my purse. Oh, we need coffee. Where should I go?"

"Take a left up here. There's a Dunkin' Donuts that's still open."

"I love their coffee."

"Me, too."

Ellen bought five coffees at the drive-thru, along with a dozen donuts, and then headed to Jacinda's place. Jacinda ran in for a carton of eggs, two small bags of ice, and a bottle of Ibuprofen.

"I brought ice for you, too," Jacinda said as she returned to the rental.

"Thanks." Ellen quickly swallowed down the Ibuprofen.

Then, she circled around to the Visitor's Center, and they rushed on foot to Peyton Randolph House.

As they approached the front door, Ellen slipped and dropped the coffees.

"Hells, bells," she said irritably.

Jacinda, who'd been carrying her cup, said, "I'll give him mine. It'll be fine. Are you okay?"

"I will be. Let's get this over with."

When they reached the first-floor parlor, they found Vernon in the corner of the sofa where they'd left him, but he was tied at the wrists and ankles and was wide awake. Sue, who stood over him, turned to Ellen as she entered.

"What the heck?" Ellen groaned.

"He was going to leave," Sue said defensively. "What took you so long?"

"You don't want to know." Jacinda handed a bag of ice to Tanya, along with a couple of Ibuprofen.

"Thanks," Tanya said.

Jacinda put the cup of coffee to Vernon's lips. "It's hot, so sip carefully."

Vernon did as she said. "That's delicious." He drank several more sips.

Ellen handed Tanya the rattle. "Ready to begin?"

"Bloody hell. I won't begin anything until I'm untied," Vernon demanded.

Ellen leaned over him and waved a finger in his face. "Then we'll leave you tied up forever! We'll leave you in the basement to rot."

"You wouldn't do that to your friend."

"Try me!" Ellen shouted. "I've gone too far to stop now."

"I should have left you in that lunatic's cellar," Vernon spat.

Ellen's mouth dropped open.

"That's right," Vernon began. "Who do you think told Eve to tell this one." He motioned toward Jacinda.

Jacinda put the cup of coffee to his lips. "Drink."

He gladly obeyed.

As Vernon drank his coffee, Sue took the candles from her purse and set them on a table beside the sofa before lighting them.

Ellen used the flame from one of Sue's candles to light the sage smudge stick. Then she blew it out and allowed the smoke to bathe over Vernon and the rest of them. Tanya shook the rattle.

Sue chanted, "Nah-tama-key-win."

"I banish all negative energy from the room," Ellen said, without thinking that she might banish Henry, too. She decided not to repeat the words, and instead, continued to wave the smudge stick in the air. "Vernon, please say the words required to break the curse."

"Untie me," he said.

Jacinda stepped back and looked as though she wanted to throw the rest of the coffee into the spiritualist's face. Ellen thought it wasn't a bad idea. But before she could suggest it, Vernon twisted his body and put his own hands in one of the flames of Sue's candles.

"Ahhh!" he shrieked. "What are you doing?"

"Getting you to cooperate," Vernon replied to Henry. "I bet you aren't used to physical pain—not like I am."

"You're bluffing, spiritualist," Henry accused. "You can take it about as well as I can. I can see your thoughts, too."

Vernon twisted and put his fingers to the flame, screaming, "Ahhhhh!"

Ellen gasped, not sure what to do. Tanya and Sue had stopped rattling and singing, so she urged them to continue.

Then, Vernon shouted, "I ask the Creator to please disarm all curses on this house."

"Say it in Powhatan, Henry!" Jacinda demanded.

When Vernon said nothing more, he moved to put his fingers toward the flame. Before his fingers touched the fire, however, he shouted, "Keshowse, nowwuntamen nkewah yohacan!"

Then, Vernon cried, "Get the egg!"

Jacinda quickly opened the carton of eggs and plucked one out.

She handed it over to Vernon, who held it with the fingers of the hand that hadn't been burned and said, "Creator, please disarm all curses and harmful devices in this house and render them destroyed. What cannot be destroyed, please release into this egg."

Then, Vernon moved the fingers of his free hand into the flame and screamed, "Ahhhh! Keshowse, nowwuntamen nkewah yohacan! Nekut meecher nkewah umpsquoth!"

Vernon sat up and handed the egg back to Jacinda. "Break it in the sink and wash it down the drain. Quickly!"

Jacinda rushed from the room with the egg. Tanya continued to shake the rattle and Sue to chant, "Nah-tama-key-win."

As they did, Vernon shouted, "I now claim every spiritual blessing that comes from the Creator. I claim them for this house and for this vessel. Allow only blessings—no curses and no entities that do not belong." Before his hands reached the flame, he said, "Nimatew ninge nus yough, Keshowse. Nimatew kewa yohacan yah musqua vunamun! Nakatew! Nakatew!"

Ellen watched in horror as Vernon writhed on the sofa.

"What's happening?" Tanya cried.

"I don't know!" Ellen leaned over the man, wondering if she should untie him or hold him down.

The whites of Vernon's eyes were showing. Then, just as Jacinda returned to the room, his body went limp.

"Vernon?" Sue put a hand on the spiritualist's forehead.

He opened his eyes and muttered, "I'm okay. My fingers hurt, but I'm okay."

"Take this ice." Jacinda handed him one of the bags of ice, originally meant for Ellen.

He held it to his fingers. Tanya stopped shaking the rattle and leaned forward in her chair.

"What happened to Henry?" Sue wanted to know. "Is he gone?"

"Not gone, but gone from me and this house," he assured her.

Ellen gave her friends a look of surprise. "That's amazing. How did you do it?"

"I tricked him into banishing himself."

"That's incredible!" Tanya praised. "Thank goodness!"

"What about the ghosts who are trapped here?" Jacinda asked. "Are they gone?"

"Some," Vernon began. "But others need help. Shall we help them to cross over, ladies?"

Tears welled in Ellen's eyes. She noticed the same was true for the others as they lifted their prayers up to God to send angels to guide the lost souls to their eternal peace.

Later, after dropping Jacinda at her place and Vernon at his, Ellen and her friends returned to the house on Kestrel Court exhausted. Tanya was still limping, and her ankle had swelled to the size of an orange despite the ice. Ellen's knees were sore, but she was otherwise fine. Sue helped her get Tanya inside.

Standing at the threshold, Ellen repeated what she'd said before: "You cannot follow us inside."

She was in the process of pouring the salt along the entry when she heard a voice in the night air say, "Boo!"

CHAPTER TWENTY

Angels

"Who's there?" Ellen said to the darkness.

"What's wrong?" Sue asked from where she and Tanya stood behind her just inside the house.

"I heard a voice. It said, *Boo*."

The porchlight flickered overhead before going out.

"Is that you, Henry?" Ellen asked.

The porchlight flickered again, and this time remained on.

Ellen entered the house and shut and locked the door. "We're not rid of him yet."

Moseby greeted her by running through her legs and putting his paws on her shins.

"You need to go outside, Moseby-Mo?"

First, she and Sue helped Tanya to the couch in the family room.

"I'm going to walk Mo outside for a bit," Ellen said. "Be right back."

"I'll make a fire," Sue offered.

Tanya cocked her head to the side. "This late?"

"I won't be able to sleep for a while—not after that," Sue argued.

"Me, either," Ellen agreed. "Should I put the tea kettle on? Would anyone else drink hot tea?"

Tanya yawned. "I would love some."

Ellen quickly filled the kettle and put it on the stove before taking Moseby out to the back to the edge of the woods. Even though Sam and the others had found their peace, she knew Henry was around, and it made her nervous. He likely resented being tricked and exorcised from Vernon. Hopefully, he wouldn't retaliate. It was atonement he was after. She hoped he remembered that.

Once the tea and the fire were made, Ellen sat with Mo and her friends in the family room by the hearth processing what they'd just experienced. They agreed that the feeling of helping the trapped souls to move on was greater than the pain and aggravation they'd endured. They hoped Vernon Blake felt the same—he was the one with the burnt fingertips.

"What are we going to do about Henry?" Tanya asked after a while.

"That should be printed on a T-shirt," Sue declared, "as often as we've said it these past months."

"Let's check in with Bob in the morning," Ellen suggested. "We don't have to wait on his team to finish their excavation, right? We can still perform our crossover ceremony tomorrow evening."

"I don't see why not," Sue agreed. "Then, maybe we can spend our last few days here actually enjoying the holidays."

Tanya grinned. "Wouldn't that be nice?"

Ellen suddenly jumped to her feet. "I just got an idea. Let's put up a Christmas tree. We can put it in the front living room by the window. I want to decorate it with bells—one bell for each of Henry's victims—to symbolize that they've moved on, that they've become angels."

Sue clapped her hands. "I love it! Like from *It's a Wonderful Life*!"

"'Every time a bell rings, an angel gets his wings,'" Ellen quoted.

"Let's do it!" Tanya agreed.

The next morning, the boulder that Sue had ordered for the front garden was delivered by way of a front-end loader. The landscaper who had created the memorial had been recommended by their contractor, Jacob. Ellen, Tanya, and Sue watched from the front porch as Steven, the landscaper, carefully drove the tractor up the drive and turned before lowering the front-end loader and slowly nudging the stone into place in the front garden.

Once it was on the ground. Steve parked the tractor and used ropes and chains to shimmy the stone into the precise position, with the etched names of those who had died face up.

"It's beautiful," Tanya said from the porch.

Although the swelling in her ankle had gone down, it was still a little sore. But she was sure it wasn't serious.

Sue and Ellen bent over the rock.

Sue read, "In July of 1778 near this very spot, thirty-nine Americans died for their country."

"Oh, look. There's Sam's name," Ellen said, moving her finger along the etching. "He made thirty-nine."

"Yes. That explains why the ghosts confused us in the beginning about how many there were. There were thirty-nine of them, but one was missing, making thirty-eight."

As she read the memorial's text, Ellen felt a sense of joy at the names of her Frost relatives. She was also reminded that Henry had not yet shared her father's message with her.

"We need memorials at Freedom Park and Jolly Pond," Sue stated.

"But there's very little chance we'll ever know the names of those victims," Ellen pointed out.

"Even so, we can still have plaques made stating that American settlers were scalped and killed and left in a mass grave."

"Or maybe not so graphic—just that they died on this spot defending America," Ellen suggested.

"I wonder whose approval we'd need to get that done."

"I bet Bob would know."

"Let's call him right after we check on Vernon," Tanya suggested. "He may need a ride to get his car."

"Sounds like a plan." Sue said. "I'll call Vernon now and offer to take him to breakfast."

"Bob might want to meet us," Ellen said. "I'll call him while you call Vernon."

By nine o'clock, Ellen and her friends were sitting at a large corner booth with Vernon and Bob at a restaurant called Another Broken Egg Café. Ellen had insisted on paying the tow bill when they'd retrieved Vernon's car on the way over. Bob had brought his students along to the restaurant, but they'd preferred to sit at their own table, which made for easier conversation, anyway.

Bob was tall and thin—except for a round pot belly—and had a receding hairline of white tufts and a short white beard. His stunning blue eyes and contagious smile had captivated Ellen when she'd first met him over six years ago. Despite what he knew about her and her friends' paranormal investigations, he was gobsmacked by their recount of the previous night. The burns on the tips of Vernon's fingers provided haunting support to their story. After the horrendous tale of the night's events, Sue shared her ideas for memorials. Bob loved Sue's idea of marking the mass graves at Freedom Park and Jolly Pond with memorial plaques. He had connections at William and Mary University and agreed to pull strings to get the memorials made and put in place.

"I was thinking the one at Freedom Park would look nice on the railing of that wooden bridge that goes over the swamp," Sue explained just as their plates were being served.

"Yes," Tanya agreed. "That's the perfect spot . . . oh, yes, the fried eggs and potatoes are mine."

"And maybe we could have a memorial bench built for the bank of Jolly Pond," Ellen suggested. "That would be better than a boulder or a plaque on a stand. People could sit and gaze out at the pond and remember Henry's victims."

"Those are my waffles," Sue said to their server.

"I love it," Bob said. "I'll get someone on that right away." To the server, he said, "Thanks, dear," when she put his omelet in front of him.

"I had the blueberry bread French toast," Vernon said to the server. "And she had the mixed berry pancakes." He pointed to Ellen.

"Thank you," Ellen said to their server.

"We need to discuss the crossover ceremonies," Sue pointed out as their server left. "Would it interfere with your plans, Bob, if we do them this evening?"

"We don't work in the dark," Bob replied. "In fact, the only reason we aren't out there this morning is because it's Sunday. We usually get a later start on Sundays. Tomorrow, we'll be back on site at the crack of dawn."

"I'd love to help, if you'll have me," Vernon said to Ellen of the crossover ceremonies.

Ellen put a hand on his shoulder. "We would love that."

That afternoon, after looking back over their recordings for the number of victims Henry had said were at Colby Swamp (twenty-six) and Jolly Pond (forty-three), Ellen did the math and calculated that they needed to buy 108 bell ornaments to represent the victims from all three mass graves. First, they drove to the Second Street Bistro for soup and salad and then headed to the outlet mall at Williamsburg Crossing for a tree, bells, and other Christmas tree trimmings.

While they were shopping, Tanya asked, "Shouldn't we do something to memorialize the ghosts from Peyton Randolph House? I feel bad that we aren't."

"I'm sure they were already memorialized by their loved ones," Sue pointed out. "Their bodies were never lost, remember? Their souls were just trapped by the curse."

"That's right," Tanya said. "And Henry's victims never got that."

"Not until now," Ellen reminded her. "We're giving them what they should have had all along."

Together, they chose a flocked tree with just enough green branches showing through the artificial snow. And, because they needed a big tree to accommodate 108 ornaments, they chose a ten-foot tall and very wide tree. They scheduled it to be delivered to the house, so they wouldn't have to mess with it themselves, and then they combed the other stores for the bells and other decorations.

Ellen felt like she'd hit the jackpot when she found a shop full of silver bell ornaments. "Aren't these perfect?"

"They are," Sue agreed, "but do you think they have 108 of them?"

The lady behind the counter asked if she could help them. When asked, she said she did not have 108 in silver, but she carried the same bells in gold and copper and together had more than enough to meet their order."

"We'll take them!" Ellen said gleefully.

Tanya, who still walked with a limp, hobbled over from across the store holding a gorgeous three-toned star in her hand. "Look at this! Silver, gold, and copper! It's perfect for the topper!"

"Oh, it is!" Sue agreed.

"You're a poet and didn't know it," Ellen laughed gayly.

They also found tiny, twinkling copper lights and added them to their pile.

"Tapered candles for the crossovers," Sue reminded them as she put a box on the counter with their decorations.

"That's a box of two dozen," Tanya pointed out. "Do we need that many?"

"Bob said he's bringing his team," Sue replied.

"And Jacinda might show up with her choir," Ellen added.

"Then we'd better get *two* boxes," Tanya said with a laugh.

"We should invite everyone over after the ceremonies," Sue said. "Maybe they'd enjoy helping us trim the tree."

"That sounds like the perfect way to end the evening," Tanya agreed.

They stopped by a grocery store on the way home to pick up a deli tray, a cracker and cheese tray, a fruit tray, and the ingredients for eggnog.

At five thirty that evening, dusk had already fallen as Ellen and her friends gathered with their guests on the bridge over Colby Swamp in Freedom Park. They began by lighting one tapered candle and passing the flame around until all their candles sparkled in the approaching nightfall. Then Ellen, who held Moseby close to her in his cloth pooch carrier, used an incense diffuser to bathe the area with the smoke of incense. While she did so, Vernon shook his rattle and sang a Native American song.

When Vernon had finished, Ellen said, "Thank you all for coming. We're here tonight to honor early Americans who died while defending our young nation. Their lives were taken under the orders of Lieutenant-Governor Henry Hamilton by Native Americans loyal to the British crown. These heroes were mercilessly killed and scalped and left to die in a heap in this swamp. They were forgotten by history until now. Please pray with me for God's heavenly angels to guide these lost souls to their eternal rest. As we say our silent prayers, let's think on those early Americans and what they sacrificed as they refused to back down from the dangers of revolution. I also call out to those spirits now, to the souls of those lost here, to please look for a light—a light brighter than that created by our burning candles. Look for God's heavenly light as we sing for your peace."

Ellen gave Jacinda a nod, who then lifted her voice into the quiet night, "Silent Night, Holy Night . . ." The rest of her twelve-member choir joined her in song, sounding like angels on earth. Tears formed in Ellen's eyes from the beauty of their singing and the beauty of their mission. She and the others soon joined the chorus, singing, "Sleep in heavenly peace. Sleep in heavenly peace."

Along with the sound of their voices lifting into the sky came the feeling of souls lifting, too. Up, up, and away they went, twinkling like stars in the dark sky.

By eight o'clock, the party had repeated their ceremony at Jolly Pond and were caravanning to the house on Kestrel Court, where they shared eggnog and grazed from the food trays which Sue had displayed on her beautiful butcher block countertops. The dining room table, on the other hand, had been spread with the little bell ornaments which, after the copper lights had been threaded onto the tree, were added one by one by everyone there.

"A bell for each soul," Ellen reminded them as they placed them on the tree.

Jacinda and her choir sang Christmas carols as everyone chipped in with the trimming of the tree. Then, once their masterpiece was done, they sang a few more songs together gathered around their gorgeous creation.

After everyone had left and Ellen and her friends and Moseby were alone once again, they were tidying up in the kitchen when Ellen heard the water turn on in the kitchen sink. She turned to see steam rising from the basin. Moments later, a message appeared in the condensation on the window over the sink. It read, *Tell Jody he was right, but I had two very good reasons why. Sorry I wasn't around more. I'm here for you now. Love, Dad.*

Ellen gazed at it, speechless.

"Oh, Ellen!" Tanya cried. "It's the message from your father!"

"It's a Christmas miracle," Sue said with tear-filled eyes.

Tanya took her phone from her trouser pocket and snapped a photo. "I'll send it to you, so you'll always have it."

Sue put an arm around Ellen's waist. "I'm so happy for you. But what does it mean?"

While Ellen understood the last part of the message, she didn't know what to make of the first part. As tears streamed down her cheeks, she found her phone and called her brother.

Sue turned off the water in the sink. "Thanks for coming through for her, Henry."

"But you're still not invited in," Tanya added.

"Was it Henry who did this?" Sue wondered. "Or did Ellen's father do it?"

"Oh, I hadn't thought of that," Tanya said. "I don't know."

"Hi, Ellen," Jody said on the other end of the phone. "We're still on for Christmas at your place, right?"

"Right. That's not why I'm calling. This is going to sound strange but bear with me."

"Okay. You've got my attention."

"If I were to get a message from Dad from beyond the grave—"

"You got a message from Dad? What did he say?"

Ellen read him the words that still lingered on the window over the kitchen sink. Then she asked, "What does that first part mean, about you being right and him having two good reasons?"

Jody was silent on the other end.

"Jody?"

"I'm here. I'm here. I just can't believe it."

"Do those words mean anything to you?"

"Yes. Ellen, I—" Jody struggled through his tears. "Not long before Dad died, I said something to him in anger. I told him I didn't understand why he'd stayed with Mom all those years when they were miserable together."

Ellen sat on a chair in the breakfast nook and leaned her elbows on the glass table. She was finding it hard to breathe.

"Ellen?"

"I'm here."

"He's saying he stayed for us—for you and me."

Ellen was nodding, though her brother couldn't see it. "Yes, I get that. Oh, Jody."

She let the sobs come. Tanya and Sue rubbed her back to bring her comfort while she and Jody remembered the man who had stayed in a miserable relationship because he thought it was best for his kids.

Whether he had made the right decision mattered less than why he'd made it. He'd made it out of love for them.

"He says he's there for us now," Ellen reminded her brother. "Do you ever talk to him?"

"Not often, but I will now."

Ellen laughed. "Yeah. Me, too." Then she added, "See you at Christmas, little brother."

"See you at Christmas. Love ya, Sis."

"Love you, too."

Ellen ended the call and wept.

Two months later, Ellen and her friends returned to Williamsburg once more to testify in the trial of Mark Murphy, who was found guilty by a jury of his peers and sentenced to ten years in a federal prison. Despite that unpleasantness, Ellen and her friends made good use of their visit. They took down their Christmas tree, put away the ornaments and, most importantly, cast their eyes on the memorials Bob had erected at Freedom Park and Jolly Pond. Bob wasn't in town, but Ellen, Sue, and Tanya invited Vernon and Jacinda to join them to view the memorials and have dinner afterward at the Fat Canary.

They also interviewed a few property management firms and selected one to take care of the house on Kestrel Court. In the evenings after eating out, they returned to the house and enjoyed the hot tub and the fireplace in the sunroom. Ellen had missed the house and was glad for another chance to visit. She and her friends hoped to visit once a year, if possible.

On the flight home to San Antonio, however, Tanya insisted that they needed a ghost-free summer vacation together, somewhere on a beach, and she'd already found the perfect place.

Showing her phone to her friends, she said, "Check out this historic house near the beach in Biloxi. Think about it: the beach during the day, the casinos at night. Wouldn't it be a fun getaway?"

"I'm sold," Sue said. "Ellen?"

"Count me in. Summer house in Biloxi, here we come!"

***

THE END

Thank you for reading my story. I hope you enjoyed it! If you did, please consider leaving a review. Reviews help other readers to discover my books, which helps me.

Please visit my website at evapohler.com to get the next book, *Summer House Mystery*.

EVA POHLER

Eva Pohler is a *USA Today* bestselling author of over thirty novels in multiple genres, including mysteries, thrillers, and young adult paranormal romance based on Greek mythology. Her books have been described as "addictive" and "sure to thrill"—*Kirkus Reviews*.

To learn more about Eva and her books, and to sign up to hear about new releases and sales, please visit her website at https://www.evapohler.com.

Printed in Great Britain
by Amazon

16223846R00118